"I can't give myself to you without a ring on my finger. I'm sorry."

Gianni's mouth curved and his forehead creased in understanding. "No need to apologize. If you have morals then you must stick by them."

"I'm so glad you understand."

"I understand perfectly. You'll only have sex with me if I marry you?"

"Yes."

"Then I accept."

"Accept what?"

"Your proposal."

"I beg your pardon?"

"Your proposal of marriage." He stepped forward and pressed her back against the wall, bringing his face so close to hers that she could practically feel the glitter burning from his eyes in her retinas. "I accept."

A Billion-Dollar Revenge

Revenge is best served...red-hot!

Ten years ago, the lives of Issy and Amelia were ruined by Gianni and Alessandro Rossi. Ever since, the Seymore sisters have plotted their revenge against the Italian billionaires. Now, it's time for Issy and Amelia to put their plan into action!

Innocent Issy will act as a distraction for playboy Gianni—then take down his company! But her attraction to him is as intense as it is unexpected... Soon, Issy's charade leads to very real vows!

After working undercover for two years at Rossi Industries, Amelia can't wait any longer for vengeance. Until she spends one incendiary night of passion with Alessandro—which has consequences! Now that she's pregnant with his child, will revenge still be what Amelia wants?

Read Issy and Gianni's story
Bound by the Italian's "I Do"
by Michelle Smart

Available now!

Read Amelia and Alessandro's story
Expecting Her Enemy's Heir
by Pippa Roscoe

Coming soon!

Michelle Smart

BOUND BY THE ITALIAN'S "I DO"

HARLEQUIN

PRESENTS

Recycling programs
for this product may
not exist in your area.

ISBN-13: 978-1-335-73920-9

Bound by the Italian's "I Do"

Copyright © 2023 by Michelle Smart

For questions and comments about the quality of this book,
please contact us at CustomerService@Harlequin.com.

Harlequin Enterprises ULC
22 Adelaide St. West, 41st Floor
Toronto, Ontario M5H 4E3, Canada
www.Harlequin.com

Printed in U.S.A.

Michelle Smart's love affair with books started when she was a baby and would cuddle them in her cot. A voracious reader of all genres, she found her love of romance established when she stumbled across her first Harlequin book at the age of twelve. She's been reading them—and writing them—ever since. Michelle lives in Northamptonshire, England, with her husband and two young Smarties.

Books by Michelle Smart

Harlequin Presents

Stranded with Her Greek Husband
Claiming His Baby at the Altar

Christmas with a Billionaire

Unwrapped by Her Italian Boss

Scandalous Royal Weddings

Crowning His Kidnapped Princess
Pregnant Innocent Behind the Veil
Rules of Their Royal Wedding Night

Visit the Author Profile page
at Harlequin.com for more titles.

This book is for the fabulous and talented
Pippa Roscoe—Pippa, thank you for making our
collaboration such a joy xxx

CHAPTER ONE

THE MESSAGE THAT pinged on Issy Seymore's phone was the notification that her taxi had been dispatched.

She met her sister's apprehensive dark eyes. This was it. Everything they'd worked towards this last decade about to come to fruition. All the late-night planning. All the scheming.

She'd imagined she'd reach this moment and be buzzing at this spring into action. She hadn't expected to feel such a weight in the belly she'd spent years working desperately hard to keep flat and toned. Gianni Rossi favoured a specific type of woman. Short brunettes that leaned towards plumpness were not in that favoured league.

'We are doing the right thing aren't we?' she whispered.

Amelia swallowed hard and nodded. 'But if you've got cold feet and want to back out then...'

'No,' she cut her off with a fortifying shake of her head. 'It's not cold feet. Just nerves, I guess.'

Amelia rubbed her arms and gave a rueful smile of understanding. If anyone understood about nerves, it was her sister. The faint bruising under her eyes was testament to the lack of sleep that had gripped them both since they'd realised five weeks ago that the stars had finally aligned and it was time to put the plan they'd spent so long finessing into action.

Amelia had taken all the risks to get them to this point, had spent two years in the enemy's camp, every minute of her working life spent with a cold knot of fear of being found out. As the Seymore sisters knew to their personal cost, the Rossi cousins were men without conscience. Without humanity. They'd ruined their lives and now it was the sisters' turn to repay the favour. Let them get a taste of what it felt to have your whole life destroyed. Because it could only be a taste. It was impossible to replicate the scale of the damage the Italian men had wrought on their family.

While Amelia had put herself on the line every working day for two years, Issy had worked safely behind the scenes, immersed in the online world. Now it was time for her to step up, step out, and play her part in the real world.

Straightening her spine, Issy stood as tall as her five-foot-one body would stretch.

Amelia's smile at this contained the first hint of humour either of them had been able to muster that day. 'Remember to keep your shoes on around him—you don't want him knowing you're short one end before you get him on the yacht.'

A splutter of laughter left Issy's lips, and she threw her arms around her big sister and hugged her tightly.

'You'll let me know as soon as you land?' Amelia asked into her hair, embracing her with equal intensity.

'I promise.'

'You've packed your charm repellent?'

She snorted and hugged her even tighter. 'You know I don't need it.'

Amelia disentangled her arms and cupped Issy's cheeks. 'Promise you'll be careful. Don't take any silly risks.'

'I won't. You be careful too.'

A shadow fell over her sister's face but she smiled. 'I'm always careful.'

Issy's phone pinged. Her driver had arrived.

One last embrace and a kiss to her sister's cheek and it was time to leave.

Time to fly to the Caribbean and put the plan they'd spent ten years strategizing into fruition.

Ten days earlier

Gianni Rossi knew when a woman was interested in him and the beautiful blonde with the fabulous legs at the bar of this ultra-exclusive, members-only club was definitely interested. She'd wafted through the swing doors with a feline grace and as she passed his table, her eyes had glanced at his. When she reached the bar, she'd turned her head to look back at him and this time the lock of her stare had not been fleeting. Now she sat sucking a cocktail through a straw with a gleam in her eye that suggested she would like to be sucking something else.

Never a man to turn down a beautiful woman blatantly showing her interest, Gianni excused himself from the company he was in. He indicated the stool beside her. 'May I?'

Wide, eminently kissable lips twitched. Dark blue eyes gleamed. 'Be my guest.'

He rested his backside on it and beckoned the barman over.

'Drink?' he asked her.

The gleam deepened. 'Sure.'

'A large bourbon for me and a…?' He raised a brow in question at her.

Dimples appeared on the beautiful face. 'Mojito. Please.'

'Mojito for the lady.'

While the barman fixed their drinks, Gianni ran his expert eye over her. Glossy shoulder length honey-blonde hair only several shades lighter than her perfectly plucked eyebrows. Beautiful elfin features. A short, silver sequinned dress with spaghetti straps that came from no high street store. A slim watch on her slim wrist from a brand also unavailable on the high street. The cut of her diamond earrings too showed that this was a woman with a discerning eye and access to an undiscerning bank account. He wondered how their paths had never crossed before.

He extended a hand. 'Gianni.'

Slim fingers wrapped around his. Her expensive, exotic perfume drifted into his space like a fragrant cloud. 'Issy.'

'I haven't seen you here before… Issy.' A name that rhymed with dizzy did not suit this sleek, confident woman with the melodious voice who pronounced her words with the same exactness as the English socialites who flocked to his parties whenever he was in London.

Gently extracting her hand from his, she flashed pretty white teeth. 'It's my first time.'

His lips curved. 'Is that a fact?'

She wiggled one of her perfect eyebrows knowingly and, enchanting blue eyes not leaving his face, closed her lips over the straw to suck the last of her original drink. The eroticism behind it sent a thrill racing through his bloodstream. Damn, this woman was *hot*.

Placing his elbow on the bar, he rested his chin on his closed hand. 'Waiting for someone?'

'My girlfriend. We're meeting here before we go to Amber's. She's running late.'

'Girlfriend?'

Amusement sparkled. 'A friend who's a girl. Why? What did you think I meant?'

He smiled slowly. 'I think you know very well what I meant.'

Another knowing, amused wiggle.

'Do you have a significant other?' he asked, cutting to the chase.

She shook her head slowly. 'Life's too short for significant others.'

A woman after his own heart. 'I couldn't agree more.'

'You're single too?'

'Always.'

'Now that is something I will gladly drink to.' Placing an elbow on the bar close to his, she mimicked him by resting her chin on her closed hand. 'So…' She tilted a little closer. 'Gianni… You're Italian?'

'*Si.*'

She grinned. 'An Italian stallion?'

How he loved a woman who knew how to use a good double entendre. 'So I've been told.'

She looked him up and down without an ounce of shame. 'I'll bet.'

Their drinks were placed before them. Gianni raised his. 'To being single.'

She clinked her cocktail to his glass, dark blue eyes bold on his. 'To having fun.' Then she pinched the straw between her thumb and forefinger and slowly inserted it between her lips. It could not be interpreted as anything but suggestive and the thrills racing through his veins ramped up.

Her phone buzzed.

'Excuse me,' she said, swiping to read the message. She replied quickly then fixed him with a rueful smile. 'That, I'm afraid, is my cue to leave.'

'Already?'

'I didn't expect to leave so soon but it's Camilla's birthday. She was going to meet me here but as she's running so late, she's got her driver to drop her at Amber's and sent him on to collect me. He'll be here in a few minutes.' She gave him an openly provocative stare, and added, 'I'm sure she won't mind if you join us.'

Gianni had been to Amber's, a tiny nightclub with a clientele comprised almost exclusively of British high society, a number of times. With regret, he waved a hand in the direction of the three men he'd not long ago abandoned. 'I'm on a poker night promise, but I can join you later…if you like?'

She finished her mojito and as she pulled the straw from her mouth, her bottom lip pulled down seductively with it. 'I do like,' she murmured, 'but I'm afraid it has to be an early night for me, midnight at the latest or I risk the danger of turning into a pumpkin.'

He rested his fingers on the hand with the immaculately manicured and painted nails that had incrementally moved closer to him and bored his gaze into hers. There was nothing he loved more than a sexy, confident woman who knew exactly what she wanted and wasn't afraid to show it, and this woman had all of that. She was sexy. Beautiful. Blonde. Long-legged. And she was unashamedly making it clear that she wanted him. The perfect temporary bedwarmer. 'I could do with an early night too.'

Her eyes gleamed and her pretty teeth grazed her bottom lip. 'As tempting as your unspoken offer is, regretfully I must decline. I'm flying to Barbados in the morning and need my beauty sleep.'

'Barbados?'

She nodded and got to her feet. 'I keep my yacht at a marina in Bridgetown. I always spend a couple of months each summer sailing.'

'Now that is a coincidence… I'm flying to the Caribbean myself in a couple of weeks.'

Her eyes widened in surprise and delight. 'Really?'

He nodded. 'We can meet up... If you like?'

She didn't even pretend to think about it. She leaned closer to whisper into his ear, close enough that her silky hair brushed against his neck. 'I would like that *very* much.' Then, smiling widely, she stepped back and pressed her phone. 'What's your number?'

He recited it to her. She entered it into her phone, then held the phone up. 'My chariot is here.'

'Then it is best you go so you don't turn into a pumpkin.'

Eyes shining, she laughed softly. 'Great to meet you, Gianni.' Then she blew him a kiss and strolled away in her fabulously high stilettos with the same ramrod-straight sexy confidence she'd entered the bar, gently curved hips swaying.

Gianni watched her leave, shaking his head and trying to stifle a laugh at what had just occurred in a few short minutes.

Ordering himself another bourbon, he re-joined his friends debating whether to throw the evening's game so he could get himself to Amber's before Cinderella turned into a pumpkin.

A moment later a message pinged into his phone.

The ball's in your court. Hopefully meet you for some fun in the Caribbean soon. Issy x

He messaged her back.

Looking forward to it. I'll be in touch. G x

* * *

Issy hailed the first black cab that passed and jumped in the back. 'Nelson Street, Brockley,' she said to the driver.

Not until the club was a blur in the distance was she able to breathe with any semblance of normality.

She'd done it.

While she kicked off the awful shoes that made her feel like her feet were clamped in vices, she fired a quick message to her sister. Amelia, she knew, would be unable to breathe properly herself until she heard from her.

It worked! Hook, line and sinker. On way home. xx

That done, she rested her head back and closed her eyes.

She felt sick. And exhilarated. And unsettled. So many emotions, all sloshing in her mostly empty stomach.

The closer the time to acting out their plans had come, the more unsettled she'd become at going through with it. When Amelia had started work at Rossi Industries, she'd vowed to find concrete proof of corruption against the cousins. They'd both needed to know that what they were doing wasn't just revenge but a good thing, that they were saving other victims from the fate their family had suffered. When Amelia had told her five weeks ago that their time had come, all Issy had been able to think was they still needed that proof. Amelia had finally found it three days ago, exultantly messaging her with the news.

The mojitos Issy had drunk suddenly rose up her throat. Pressing her hand there, she squeezed her eyes even tighter and willed the nausea to pass.

She willed even harder to banish the image of Gianni Rossi looking at her like he would gladly eat her whole.

And willed even harder than that to forget the thrills that had run through her veins to see it.

Rob Weller, one of Gianni's favourite architects and a good friend though an infuriating timekeeper, arrived at the same time the barman brought Gianni's fresh bourbon to the table.

'Man, I have just seen the hottest woman leave this place,' he enthused as he slid his short frame onto the seat across from Gianni.

'Bet that's the woman Gianni just hooked up with,' Stefan said with a knowing grin.

'We didn't hook up,' Gianni felt obliged to point out.

'I saw you give her your number.'

Gianni smiled but kept his mouth shut. While he dated widely and enthusiastically, one thing he never did was kiss and tell. Not that there had been any kissing to tell about. Just one short, incredibly flirtatious conversation…and the potential for more than flirtatious conversation.

For fifty weeks of the year, he worked his backside off. For sure, he partied hard too, but work came first. It always had. It was the same for Alessandro, his cousin and business partner. Practically raised as brothers, the Rossi cousins had been twelve when they'd determined to carve their own path in life, paths that sped them away from their monstrous fathers, and they had worked their fingers to the bone and overcome huge setbacks to make their property development company the multi-billion-euro, internationally renowned enterprise it was today. Where Gianni and Alessandro differed was on the partying side of life. Andro lived and breathed Rossi Industries. He rarely took time off. He never dated. He liked his own company so much that Gianni had long ago taken to calling him The Monk. But for all his cousin's single-minded drive and monkish ways, he understood Gianni needed to occasionally blow off steam and recharge his batteries and so had never begrudged the two weeks Gianni spent in the Caribbean each summer. That fortnight was sacrosanct, highlighted in the diary of every one of the hundred thousand Rossi Industries employees. The company would have to be burning down before Andro bothered him during it or let anyone else do so.

'Leggy blonde, wearing a skimpy silver dress?' Rob asked.

'That's the one,' Stefan agreed.

'Man…' Rob shook his head. 'I almost threw myself into the cab she hailed so she could argue with me for it.'

'Bit creepy,' Gianni pointed out.

'How else can I get a woman like that to look at me without flashing my bank account at them?' Rob defended himself. 'It's all right for you. Women don't care about the size of your wallet. You only have to look at a woman for her to want to…'

'Did you say she hailed a cab?' Gianni interrupted before his friend could say anything that might prompt a passing woman to throw a drink over his head.

'Yes.'

'There wasn't a car waiting for her?'

'No. She definitely hailed a black cab. Why?'

He shrugged and raised his glass to his mouth. 'No reason.'

Intriguing. Issy had told him her friend's driver was collecting her, which did not imply the beauty hailing a black cab.

Why the lie?

He tipped the rest of his bourbon down his throat and smiled. The only thing he loved more than a sexually confident woman was a sexually confident enigma begging to be solved.

His annual trip to the Caribbean couldn't come soon enough. If nothing else, it certainly promised to be fun.

Once Issy's stomach had settled a little, she took a deep breath and made the call.

'David?' she said when it was answered. 'It's Isabelle Seymore.'

'Issy!' he cried. She could hear music pounding in the background and guessed he was at a party somewhere. 'What can I do for you, my darling?'

'It's time.'

'Time? For what?'

'You know what. A yacht.'

There was a long pause. 'When do you need it for?'

'Next Friday.'

'That soon?'

'I did warn you that when the time came, I would need it to happen quickly.'

He sighed. 'You still need it for two weeks?'

'Yes.'

'With a full crew?'

She pinched the bridge of her nose. 'Yes. And a minimum of forty feet. As we agreed when I spent six months working for you for free.'

David liked to call himself a broker but really, he was a fixer to the rich. Want the use of a private jet for a weekend? Then David is your man. Need to throw a last-minute party on an obscure island with exquisite catering and hedonistic entertainment? Give David a call. In the mood for chartering a fully crewed superyacht? That's right—call David.

Issy had taken a six-month sabbatical from her job as an auxiliary nurse to work as David's girl Friday two years ago, when Amelia had first got the job at Rossi Industries. Six months of free labour at roughly one hundred hours a week, and all for this moment. If she hadn't once been best friends with David's little sister he'd have made her work a full year.

No one could accuse the Seymore sisters of slacking in their preparation. Or their research.

The cab pulled up outside the run-down block of flats she and Amelia called home.

Wedging her swollen feet back into the vices, she walked as gingerly as she could up the stairwell to her flat—the lift was, as always, broken—and Issy's mind drifted back to the day she'd learned monsters really did exist. She remembered it so clearly.

It had been a Sunday. Her mother had cooked a traditional English roast. Issy had been in charge of prepping the vegetables, Amelia in charge of making the batter for the Yorkshire puddings and the cheese sauce. During the meal, their parents had allowed thirteen-year-old Issy and fifteen-year-old Amelia to have a small glass of red wine each. Their parents had argued whether or not to take the girls out of school a week early so they could enjoy their Tuscan home a little longer than planned. None of them had known that in a matter of weeks the girls would be pulled out of their school permanently because the wealth that paid the fees would be gone.

When the doorbell rang, none of them had suspected what was about to happen.

Brenda, their housekeeper, was on her day off so the girls' mother, a vivid, beautiful woman with such *presence*, had answered the door. She'd returned shortly, anxiety on her face, and whispered to their father, who'd then excused himself.

Issy had just put a roast potato in her mouth when raised voices echoed from their father's study into the dining room. Without a word, the Seymore sisters and their mother slipped from the table and hovered outside it.

Male voices, heavily accented but with a precise pronunciation that meant the three of them heard every scornful, abusive word sounded through the crack in the study door.

'You're finished, old man. The sooner you accept that the better—for your sake.'

'What was yours is now ours, you washed-up, sorry excuse of a man. Accept it.'

'*Everything* is ours.'

'Everything. Say goodbye to your company…and hello to Lucifer. He's been waiting for you.'

Footsteps had neared the door. Issy and Amelia had held each other tightly as the door swung open and two tall, dark-haired men in impeccably tailored suits sauntered out of their father's study with all the swagger of a pair of gangsters in the films she was forbidden to watch. They failed to see the wife and daughters of the man they'd just ripped to shreds cowering behind the door. But the daughters had seen them.

Time had frozen. When their father finally appeared in the study doorway he'd aged two decades. The next morning, the frightened adolescent girls, who'd shared a bed that night, had woken from a fitful sleep to find his thinning dark hair had turned white overnight. A year later he was dead. A decade on, their mother was nothing but an empty shell of the vibrant woman she'd once been, distraught to wake each day, reliant on stimulants to get her out of bed.

Issy and Amelia had never been particularly close before that awful day. Close in age, yes, but nothing else. They'd have sooner scratched each other's eyes out than pay the other a compliment. That day, though, had pulled them together in a way the Rossi cousins could never have dreamed if they'd even bothered to consider the two innocent girls caught up in the collateral damage of their heinous actions. It had drawn them into a solid unit with only one purpose—revenge.

For the first time in a decade, Issy had the faint hint of what that revenge would taste like on her tongue.

CHAPTER TWO

The *Palazzo delle Feste* gleamed under the dazzling Caribbean sun. It would have dazzled Issy even if it had been raining.

Blinking back her disbelief, she looked at David's deadpan face. 'How on earth did you manage to get this for me?'

He waved an airy hand. 'Just call me a magician.'

She turned her stare back to the humungous vessel docked before her. 'A magician? David, this is way beyond anything I asked for.' Their agreement had been six months free labour in exchange for the use of a sleek, modern yacht of at least forty feet, something a young, independently wealthy or trust-funded woman would reasonably own. This yacht had to be three times that size!

Heart sinking, she shook her head. 'It's amazing but it's too much.' It was too conspicuous. How could she blend in if things went wrong and she needed to escape? Plus something this size would give the impression she was in the league of billionaires. She knew how to pull off rich—after all, her family had once been rich—but this was a whole different league. This was Silicon Valley and oligarch territory. 'I need something much smaller.'

'Sorry, darling, but no can do. We're hitting the summer season. Everything's either booked or the owners are wanting them for themselves.'

'But this isn't what we agreed.'

'Darling, I've managed to acquire one of the finest superyachts in the whole of the Caribbean for your exclusive use, and you're complaining about it? Look at her! She's a masterpiece! She's got a helipad, two swimming pools, a library, an entertainment room, a games room, a movie room, a casino, a beauty parlour, a spa, *and* she has an inflatable slide that you can swish down straight into the sea. And if all that doesn't tempt you, she has her own speedboat, Jet Skis and a load of other water sports goodies tucked away for your personal use.'

No wonder it was named the Party Palace. This was a vessel equipped and dedicated to its owner having a good time.

'Does the owner know you're giving her away for a fortnight at no charge?' Chartering something of this size and opulence complete with full crew would generally set someone back around the hundred thousand mark. Per week. In English pounds. She would have had to work for David for free for ten years to pay for this.

'Ask me no questions and I will tell you no lies.'

She fixed him with a stare that, instead of making him quail, made him laugh and throw his arms around her. 'Oh, Isabelle, Isabelle. Why so serious? You're in the Caribbean. You have a superyacht with a crew of twenty at your disposal. *Enjoy it*, my darling. Everything is taken care of. Anything you could possibly want will be provided. If you're anchored at sea and want a Methuselah of Moët flown in or a hundred white roses, ask and it shall be delivered.'

'Have you really not got anything smaller I can use?'

'Do you know what the definition of stupid is? Asking the same question again and again hoping for a different answer.'

From the other side of the harbour, standing at the balustrade of his hotel room's balcony, Gianni watched the exchange between Issy and the broker through his binoculars. His beautiful hustler did not look pleased at the broker's offering. He didn't need to be a lip-reader to know she was arguing about it. He smiled when her shoulders sagged and she finally appeared to concede defeat. He was proved right a moment later when they climbed the steps onto the *Palazzo delle Feste*. The captain joined them. She shook his hand then followed the two men inside and out of Gianni's view.

Well played, David, he thought. There was nothing in the broker's demeanour to suggest anything was amiss. The promise of a further quarter million if the con woman accepted the yacht was too big a temptation for him to want to screw this up. That money was on top of the hundred thousand Gianni had already paid him. Information came with a price, and Gianni was happy to pay it.

He sent her a message.

Just landed. Can't wait to see you. G x

How did he know she was a hustler? His gut. It was never wrong. The one time he'd ignored it, the consequences had been disastrous. The evidence was pretty damn convincing too. Beautiful woman entering a club renowned as a haven for the rich and powerful, on the lookout for a man to reel in. She'd played her part beautifully. Those come-to-bed eyes. The seductive smile. The *pièce de résistance*—her enthusiasm for the single life. Unspoken had been the promise of a no-strings-attached fling that any man would salivate for while cleverly and subtly establishing that she *was* rich by mentioning her yacht. Putting herself on an equal financial footing to quell any doubts her victim might have. She'd been *magnificent*. If Rob hadn't seen her get into a cab and establish that she'd told at least one lie, Gianni wouldn't have doubted her at all. That's how good she'd been. And if he hadn't doubted her he wouldn't have got a close associate in Barbados to ask around at all the marinas in Bridgetown about a beautiful blonde called Issy who kept her yacht moored there. No one had heard of this woman…but all the digging around did reveal one delicious nugget. The slippery English broker David Reynolds was trying to pull in a favour and borrow—not charter—a modest yacht of no less than forty feet. What made this nugget so delicious was that the notoriously greedy David lived on his own yacht so was unlikely to need it for himself.

Oh, and the date he needed it for was, coincidentally, the day Gianni flew out to the Caribbean.

On a hunch, Gianni got his associate to have a little chat with David Reynolds. After handing over considerable cold hard cash, he hit pay dirt. The yacht was needed for the exclusive use of a woman called Isabelle Clements.

It could have been a coincidence. Except Gianni didn't believe in coincidence. Only one way to find out, and that was to offer up his brand-new yacht, the *Palazzo delle Feste*, to the mysterious Isabelle Clements.

His gut and hunches had all been proved right. The beautiful Issy was indeed Isabelle Clements.

The beautiful Issy was indeed a hustler. A con woman.

His phone buzzed. The hustler had responded.

What a coincidence! Just docked! Still up for meeting at Freddo's later? x

They'd exchanged dozens of messages and numerous phone calls since their contrived meeting. It had been great fun stringing her along, asking her questions about what she was up to, wondering what outrageous lie she'd come up with next. 'Oh, I've spent the day snorkelling,' or, 'I spent the day with friends in St Lucia. Have you been? Oh, you must, it's to die for!' It was the phone calls he'd enjoyed the most, and not just because he could imagine her squirming over the lies he was forcing her to fabricate on the hoof. He kept capturing hints of genuine humour in her beautiful voice that only added to the anticipation. A hook-up with a beautiful hustler with a sense of humour? What man could resist?

He fired a quick reply.

Wouldn't miss it for the world. 5 p.m.? G x

Her response flashed moments later.

Perfect. x

He read their most recent exchange a second time and grinned.

Let the games commence.

Issy was trying very hard not to panic. She needed to entice Gianni onto 'her' yacht by tomorrow at the latest. She knew that wouldn't be a problem, but what *would* be a problem was how she'd be able to act the role of superyacht owner when she didn't know her way around said superyacht.

She could have cheerfully kicked David in the ankle for screwing this up. She'd been specific about her requirements. Six months spent as his unpaid dogs-body meant she'd earned the right to be specific about them. Issy and Amelia had spent hours debating the best kind of yacht for Issy to have, and in all honesty, a battered old fishing boat would be better than this floating palace.

Still, David had assured her the crew would lie to any guest she brought on board and say she was the owner, and all that time spent as David's dogsbody meant she knew yacht crews were meticulously trained and would cater to her every need without her having to actually open her mouth and order them about. She'd never been any good at ordering people about, mainly because she hated being bossed about herself and so cringed to hear commands come out of her own mouth.

Knowing Amelia would be worrying, she took a picture of her opulent bedroom and sent it to her. She didn't dare tell her sister about David's cock-up, but a nice internal picture that didn't give anything away would do fine. Amelia needed to focus on her own task of pushing through her recommendation of a specific company for the Rossi Industries project she was managing. In reality, that specific company was nothing like Amelia had made it appear on paper. Going with that company would be an unmitigated disaster for Rossi Industries. The knock-on effects would destroy their entire enterprise. And destroy them. Perfect.

The sisters had known for a long time that the only way to topple the Rossi cousins would be by separating them. Together, they were as solid as rock, the cousins perfectly complementing each other so that nothing ever slipped past them. It would be impossible for Amelia to succeed if both cousins had to sign the project off and with it, sign off her recommendation. One cousin might miss or overlook something but the other would always pick it up.

Divide and conquer. It was the only way for the Seymore sisters to win, and it was with that thought at the forefront of her mind that Issy forced her feet into a pair of impossibly high wedged sandals—stilettos were forbidden on this yacht—and inspected her appearance one last time. Seeing as Gianni believed she'd been in the Caribbean for ten days already, fake tan had been a necessity, and she paid special attention to her exposed flesh to ensure her skin was streak-free. Satisfied she looked as good as she could for the money she'd paid, Issy made her way out of the floating palace to meet her handsome nemesis.

Here she came, striding gracefully towards the beachside restaurant, blonde hair blowing gently in the breeze, large designer shades covering much of her beautiful face, lithe body showcased to perfection in a pale green shirt dress that skimmed her deeply golden thighs and was complemented by a large, brightly coloured beaded necklace.

He rose from his chair to greet her.

Pretty white teeth flashing in delight, she strode straight to him and rested a hand on his shoulder so they could exchange kisses to each other's cheeks. A cloud of her exotic perfume enveloped him. He inhaled it as greedily as he relished the brush of her lips against his skin.

His memories hadn't played him false. She was every inch as stunning as he remembered.

'Well, here we are,' she said brightly once she'd settled herself in the seat across from him, lifting her shades to rest on top of her head.

He smiled slowly, noting the shirt dress was unbuttoned enough to expose a glimpse of black lace bra, a deliberate tactic he was sure, and one he wholeheartedly approved of. If this was a taster of Isabelle Clements tactics for hustling money out of him then he was in for one hell of a ride. 'Here we are. I hope you don't mind but I've taken the liberty of ordering you a mojito.'

Those deep blue eyes he remembered so vividly sparkled. 'You have an impressive memory and no, I don't mind at all.'

For the longest time nothing was said as they gazed at each other, both feigning disbelief that they had actually made this happen, that they were sat across a table from each other in a restaurant located thousands of miles and numerous time zones from where they'd met.

Books had been written and films made about people like Issy Clements. Gianni cared not at all that he was the man her net had been thrown at. On the contrary. Anticipation as to how far she was prepared to go in her hustle thrummed heavily in him.

It had been a long, long time since he'd experienced excitement on a level like this. It wasn't that his life was boring—far from it—but Gianni and Alessandro had achieved such success with their business and after such torrid beginnings that there was no challenge left to it now. Nothing to strive for other than success on top of success. He would never be so immodest as to deny that Mother Nature hadn't blessed him with looks that most women found attractive but since his bank balance had sprung into the stratosphere, women had ceased to be a challenge too. Sometimes he would go to a party and have so many feminine eyes openly seduce him that he felt like a kid in a sweetshop who'd already gorged on all the chocolate. He could take his pick. And he did.

Like the cars he drove, Gianni liked his women fast, sleek and glossy; preferably tall and blonde. He also preferred them to have money, not from any form of snobbery—after all, he and his cousin came from nothing—but because he'd tired of reading about his 'sexploits' in the press. As he didn't date any woman long enough to learn if she was trustworthy or not, it made sense to shrink his dating pool to those he knew from the off didn't need to sell stories about him.

'So...' he said, breaking the silence with a seductive gleam. 'Do you come here often?'

Was it possible for the man to have a cheesier chatup line? Issy wondered, mentally rolling her eyes. He was just so sure of himself, so keenly aware of the power of his sexuality and the effect it had on women that she supposed he didn't feel the need to bother using his wit. And he had wit. A great deal of it. She knew. She'd researched the man for years, night after night spent searching his name, learning the minutest detail about him. Of course, Amelia had got to know him quite well in a professional capacity and she'd grudgingly admitted he was as good-humoured in real life as he came across in interviews and the snippets of conversation attributed to him. Most of the time, in any case. It never boded well on anyone who dared cross him...but the Seymore sisters already knew that. They'd lived it.

His rampant sexuality had no effect on her. Gianni's

handsome face, with its square jaw and the firm lips considered by many, many women to be *kissable* repulsed her. How many hours had she sat at her laptop staring into those light blue eyes with her stomach churning violently? Too many. There was not a millimetre of his face she was unfamiliar with, from the slight cleft in the tip of his broken nose—she would one day learn who broke it and shake their hand—to the way his left eyebrow sat a fraction higher than the right. She knew the dark hair currently exposed at the top of his unbuttoned black shirt whirled over defined pectoral muscles and down over a flat washboard stomach. She knew he was exactly six foot three. She knew he had his thick dark hair trimmed every fortnight. She knew that by the end of his two weeks in the Caribbean the currently stubbled square jaw would be covered in a thick black beard that would then be shaved before he returned to the world of business. She knew that if it was possible to think of Gianni dispassionately, she'd agree he was a walking shot of testosterone and that his muscular frame contained a potent sexuality that would make any other woman weak at the knees.

But not her. Issy was immune to any sexuality he exuded. The burn that had ignited in her veins in the London bar was the deep anticipation of impending revenge. The haunting of his gorgeous face in her thoughts was nothing new. He'd haunted her for years. What made the haunting bearable was imagining it crumpling the day he realised she'd taken everything he held dear from him.

Still, she'd thought better of him than cheesy chat-up lines.

Returning the gleam, she answered, 'Barbados is great, but I prefer to be out on the open sea. You?'

'Depends on my mood. When I'm on land all I require is great food, great beer and an excellent view.'

She let her gaze bore into his. 'The view from where I'm currently sitting is pretty something.'

He returned the heated stare. 'Really?'

She smiled suggestively and took great pleasure in watching his light blue eyes darken. Two years spent starving herself to create the feminine stick insect look he desired was paying off.

Her mojito and a fresh lager for Gianni was brought to their table. He held his bottle aloft. 'To the start of a beautiful new friendship.'

Smiling, Issy clinked her glass to it and took a flirtatious sip of her cocktail through the straw.

'I have to say, your command of the English language is seriously impressive,' she said, stroking his ego. 'If it wasn't for the hint of an accent, you could believe it was your first language.' A decade ago, his accent had been strong. 'Were you raised bilingual?'

'I'm self-taught.'

'Even more impressive. What spurred you on?'

'My business is based in England. I run it with my cousin.'

'What kind of business?'

'Property. What business are you in?'

'I'm not—I'm a trust fund baby.'

'Rich mummy and daddy?'

Ignoring the faint mocking tone of his voice, she nodded and had another drink.

'And what do Mummy and Daddy do?'

She told him the first real truth of their acquaintance. 'Daddy died quite a few years ago and Mummy's in rehab.'

Gianni made a suitably sympathetic face. So *this* was how the hustle was going to work. Personally, he would have put his money on her letting slip about a seriously ill close family member—a small niece or nephew would be ideal—whose life was hanging in the balance but who could be saved if only they could afford the excruciating amount of money needed for a proven but experimental treatment that poor Issy would love to pay herself if not for a temporary cash-flow problem. Mummy being in rehab was less heart-rending but, on reflection, a safer bet. No medical jargon to remember.

He mentally applauded her for sowing the seed so early, and made another private bet to himself that by the end of the evening she would have mentioned the excruciating costs of the rehab facility.

'That must be tough for you.'

'What doesn't kill you makes you stronger,' the clever hustler dismissed airily.

He raised his beer. 'I will drink to that.'

Clinking bottle to glass again, they finished their drinks. While they waited for fresh ones to be brought over, Issy scoured the menu searching for the meal that contained the least amount of calories.

When this was all over, she was going to hit her favourite fast-food restaurant and bury her face in all the burgers and chips and ice cream she'd spent the last two years denying herself.

She ordered a low-fat Caesar salad and made sure not to sound like she was ordering her personal equivalent of dog food.

'What does a trust fund baby do all day?' he asked once their order had been taken.

She fluttered her eyelashes. 'Why, has fun of course.'

'And where do you like to have your fun?'

Smiling suggestively, she wrapped a lock of hair around her finger in the same way she'd noted a couple of his old lovers had done. 'That all depends.'

'On?'

'My mood… And the company.'

Eyes gleaming, he laughed. 'Has anyone told you you're beautiful?'

I should ruddy hope I look beautiful, Cheesy Chat-Up Man. It cost a ruddy fortune to achieve this look.

Until exactly two weeks ago, when Amelia found the proof they'd been seeking and they'd realised the stars had finally aligned for them, Issy had rarely worn make-up, never bothered with fake tan and her hair had been a lank dark chestnut normally shoved back in a ponytail or plait.

'Has anyone told you you're an incredibly sexy man?'

He leaned forwards, wafting his cologne with him. 'Not in the last ten days.'

Been slacking, have you? Or too busy with the Au-

*rora project that's about to come to fruition for Rossi
Industries and is worth billions to you? Or so you think.*

'Have you been hiding in a cave?'

He grinned. 'Not quite. Work has been all consum-
ing. Believe me, I've earned this break.'

*You certainly have. Earned it off the grave of my fa-
ther when you forced a hostile takeover of his company.*

'A week to unwind and recharge your batteries?'

'Two weeks.'

'Two?' She raised one of the eyebrows she'd plucked
into submission, as if she didn't know exactly when
he was due to return to what would be left of his business. 'How much fun can one man have in two weeks?'

'That all depends.'

'On?'

'If there's someone for me to play with.'

She held his gaze and smiled. 'Oh, I imagine a man
like you would have no shortage of playmates.'

'It's never been a problem for me before.'

Such modesty. It was so becoming. Not.

'You know, my yacht has many toys on board.'

The sexy gleam shimmered. 'Really?'

'Uh-huh.' Emulating his gleam, she mimicked him
further by leaning forwards, deliberately allowing him
a good peek of her cleavage. 'I even have a slide.'

'Who doesn't love a good slide on a yacht?'

She grazed her teeth over her bottom lips and
dropped her voice to a seductive purr. 'My thoughts exactly. If you haven't got anything planned, how would
you like to join me on it tomorrow? We can take it to
sea…try the slide out.'

'I can think of nothing I'd rather do.'

She raised her glass and flashed her first genuine smile. 'It's a date.'

He practically stripped her naked with his eyes. 'I'm already looking forward to it.'

CHAPTER THREE

Issy examined every inch of her bikini-clad body. The last time she'd worn a swimsuit she'd been twelve and forbidden from wearing anything but a full-piece swimsuit by her protective parents. She had a feeling if either of them could see the teeny-weeny white bikini she was wearing now, they would spontaneously combust.

She was scared she might spontaneously combust too, in embarrassment.

But this was the kind of bikini Gianni Rossi's lovers wore. She couldn't afford to disappoint him until they were far out at sea and she'd managed to throw his phone overboard.

But, heavens, it was revealing. Luckily it covered her bottom half quite well apart from where it tied together at the side of her hips, but about the only thing it covered up top was her nipples.

Feeling the panic that often tried to grab her throat rise, Issy breathed deeply and wrapped a sheer blue sarong around her to give herself the illusion of modesty. It was too late to back out now.

She only had to lead him on until she got rid of his phone, and then she could dress herself in a sack if she so pleased.

The problem was she could taste danger. It had been there on her tongue since she woke that morning. She had no idea where it was coming from, but her Spidey senses were warning her of *something*.

Warning her of Gianni? And if so, why?

Was she playing with fire?

Gianni was a playboy, but he was not a man to force a woman. None of his legion of lovers had a bad word to say about him and there was no way Amelia would have gone along with this if she'd thought Issy would be putting herself in any kind of physical danger with him. As she'd grudgingly put it, he was gentleman playboy.

Issy's gut had aligned with Amelia's description of him during their first meet in London. Her gut told her he posed no physical danger to her. So why did she feel so threatened? Was it even threatened that she was feeling?

Too late now. Today was the day Amelia made her bogus recommendation to Alessandro Rossi and the rest of the team. Issy needed to get Gianni out to sea and keep him there, without communication, until she had word that the contracts were signed and the deal that would destroy the Rossi cousins was done. That should take around three days but could be longer. She would have to flirt. Lead him on. Maybe allow him a kiss or two…and trust her sister and her own gut that he wouldn't force those simple kisses or two into anything more.

Heaven help her, she'd never led a man on before.

Truth was, she'd barely been kissed either. Her one barely kiss had occurred when she'd been David's dogsbody, by one of his caterers. Unfortunately said caterer had been handling fish and the smell oozing from him had put her off so much that she'd spent the rest of her dogsbody career avoiding him. There had been no one else. Between her real day job in the children's ward and her night job of learning everything there was to know about Gianni, there had been no time for anyone else. Besides, it was a bit hard to look at men in a romantic way when your thoughts were consumed by someone else, even if that was someone you despised with a passion, and she hated that she'd relaxed into his company over their meal and that the hours had passed so quickly. He'd regaled her with tales of his friends' exploits that had genuinely amused her. If she didn't know who he was, she would be in danger of actually liking him.

But that was the power of the man. Beneath the handsome, easygoing exterior, Gianni was the devil in disguise.

Straightening her spine, she left her bedroom and made her way to the deck Gianni would enter 'her' yacht from. After their meal, she'd spent a couple of intense hours familiarising herself with the main areas of the yacht and felt a lot more confident about passing it off as her own than she had when David had shocked her with it.

Two crew members were already on deck, ready to greet her guest.

Issy was about to take a seat in the shaded section when a tall figure emerged dockside in the distance.

Her heart and belly did a simultaneous flip.

The closer he strolled, the harder her heart pumped.

Even though he wore shades as large as her own, he still turned heads from both sexes. Maybe it was the black polo shirt he wore, which fit snugly across his broad chest and showcased his spectacular physique. Or maybe it was the canvas khaki shorts that she knew without having to check showcased his tight butt cheeks.

He stopped a few feet from the yacht, looking as if he were reading its name to make sure he'd reached the right one, then caught sight of her. A devastating smile stretched across his face and he bounded up the right-hand steps to board.

Her heart pumped even harder and faster.

'*Bella*, your yacht is as dazzling as you are,' he said as he closed in on her and laid a hand on her hip. He kissed both her cheeks before taking her hand and bringing it to his mouth. He grazed his lips over her knuckles. 'A stunning vessel for a stunning lady.'

To her absolute horror, Issy felt a burn crawl over her cheeks and knew she was blushing. Or was that flushing? Because she didn't know if it was the heat of his breath on her skin causing it or the seductive appreciation in his stare.

'I enjoy my time on it,' she murmured, hoping her own huge shades covered enough of her face to disguise the flush.

'I can imagine. Her name tells me you're a lady who lives to party.'

She bestowed him with a knowing smile and slowly extracted her manically tingling fingers from his hold. 'Today, the party is just you and me. Drink?'

He checked his thick watch and raised a neat black eyebrow. 'Too early for champagne?'

'It's never too early for champagne.' She nodded at one of the hovering crew, who bowed his head in answer and disappeared to sort the drinks for them, then turned to the other one. 'Tell the captain we're ready to set sail.'

Subtly bracing herself first, Issy tucked her hand into the crook of Gianni's muscular arm. 'That's if you're happy for us to set sail?'

Removing his shades, he practically stripped her naked with his hungry stare. 'I am at the mercy of your every whim.'

The sensation of being under threat hit her so hard that she had to grind her toes into her impossibly high wedged sandals to stop her feet running and throwing herself overboard. The flesh of Gianni's arm was warm beneath her hand. Smooth. A texture completely different to her own. The tingling in her fingers seeped through her skin and into her bloodstream, making her already frantic beating heart increase in tempo. There was nothing fake about the breathlessness of her voice when she managed to tease, 'Oh, I do love it when a man's at my mercy.'

Eyes alight with sensuality, he wolfishly, playfully, snapped his teeth together. The tingles in her blood seeped even lower. Deeper. Her legs had become distinctly wobbly.

They'd barely stepped inside when Danny, who'd worked for Gianni for six years, carried their champagne over, holding the tray out and not betraying by so much as a flicker that he knew him.

'Thank you,' the con woman said. 'Please tell Chef we will want lunch on the pool deck in an hour.'

Gianni didn't try to stop the swelling laughter. His head chef, whose name she'd clearly not learned, was called Christophe and had worked for him for even longer than Danny. This was all just too delicious.

Seeing Issy's curious stare, he merely held his glass out so they could make yet another clink, tipped half the champagne he himself had paid for down his throat, then took hold of her free hand and leaned his face close to her ear. She was wearing that wonderful perfume again and, having twisted her blonde hair into a chic knot, he could smell the underlying sweetness of her skin layered in it. For perhaps the hundredth time, he allowed his imagination to run riot as to how far Isabelle Clements was prepared to go in her hustle. He could only hope she would go far enough that he got to inhale more of her scent than the delicate arch of her neck. 'Show me around your party palace.'

The quiver of her skin was so subtle he could easily have missed it. But he didn't miss it. He saw it. He felt it.

He smiled.

This just got better and better. His hustler genuinely desired him. Since realising she was a con woman, he'd wondered if she'd targeted him deliberately—Gianni was well-known in the media and the club she'd turned up at was one he was known to frequent—or if any man there that night who'd caught her eye would have done. He didn't suppose it mattered. But it did make the game a lot more fun to suspect a genuine desire on her part.

As Gianni had yet to spend any real time in his new yacht, it was quite surreal to be given a tour of it by the great pretender. Everything had been designed with his input. The fact all the entertainment, from the casino to the movie room, was confined to the main deck was deliberate, and when they reached the games room with the full-size snooker table he couldn't resist raising a querying eyebrow. He suspected that when those heels were removed, Issy would reveal herself to be much shorter than she carried herself. Snooker was by no means a man's game but it helped to be able to see over the table. 'You're a snooker player?'

'Some of my guests like to play,' she neatly deflected. 'I'm not known as the hostess with the mostest for nothing.'

He grinned. She might be a con woman but beneath the high-society persona she was playing for all its worth he thought might lurk a woman who was genuinely fun. 'Want to play?'

'And miss out on the sunshine? We can play when the sun goes down.'

'You're not going to return me to shore before you turn into a pumpkin?'

Her dimples appeared—a sign he was starting to

recognise meant she was genuinely amused. 'Want to swim?'

'Does that mean I get to go on your slide?'

Stepping closer to him, she picked a speck of flint off his polo shirt and huskily said, 'That all depends.'

He rested a hand on her hip. The gap between them was so small he could feel the heat of her hot body. 'Depends on what?'

Her teeth grazed her bottom lip and her eyes gleamed. 'On where we anchor, of course.' A smile lit her face and she tugged at his hand. 'Come on, I want to swim before we eat.'

Issy discreetly checked her watch as she removed it. The meeting in London would be well under way. Casually, she placed the watch with her phone on the table and made sure not to react when Gianni placed his own watch and phone next to them, then added his wallet to the pile.

She just needed to keep him off that phone until the moment to get rid of it presented itself...

Pondering on how to dispose of it dissolved when Gianni pulled off his polo shirt.

Suddenly she was overcome with the need to fan herself. Dear God in heaven, that body...

That thought dissolved too when his hands went to the button of his canvas shorts.

Her mouth ran dry.

It hadn't occurred to her until that precise moment that Gianni hadn't brought anything with him other than what was laid on the table.

The zip went down. Eyes locked on her face, his hands went to his hips and he tugged the shorts down.

Issy caught a glimpse of thickened hair at the base of his abdomen…at his groin…before the shorts fell to the floor and, with the hint of a wink, he casually pulled up the swim shorts he was wearing beneath them to a more modest level.

'Do you have sun cream?' he asked.

'Sorry?' she croaked.

'Sun cream. You know, the stuff you cover your skin with to stop you burning and hopefully prevent you from getting a melanoma?'

Pull yourself together! she shouted at herself. *You've seen his body before, many, many times.*

But, dear God in heaven, it was one thing to see that body on a laptop screen and quite another to see it in the flesh.

No picture, however talented the photographer, could do that body justice. Or that face.

'Yes.' That was better. More normal. She pulled a smile to her face and took out the expensive sun cream from the bag that had cost her two weeks' wages, and handed it to him. She was struck, not for the first time, by the size and strength of his hands, and fresh tingles zipped through her skin and veins to imagine those hands…

To imagine those hands *what*? Touching her?

Had she already had too much sun? Because she was fast starting to think her brain had become addled. There was no reason on earth for her to imagine that, just like there'd been no reason on earth for the heat that had pulsed through her when she'd picked at the imaginary fleck on his polo shirt a while ago, or for that heat to deepen in her most intimate part when his hand had rested on her hip and only the sheerness of her sarong had been a barrier between their flesh. No reason for that moment when anticipation had thrummed through her at the thought of his firm lips closing on hers.

Issy had a job to do. This man was her enemy. If her body was developing signs that could be mistaken for attraction then she had to rise above them. No way it was attraction. No way Jose.

'Would you do my back for me?' he asked once he'd finished slathering every inch of his limbs and torso.

Absolutely not!

'My pleasure,' she purred, taking the bottle from him and resisting squirting it in his eyes.

Standing behind him, she controlled the urge to squirt it cold straight onto his naked skin and dolloped a load into her hand.

Holding her breath, she put her hands to his back.

The muscles bunched.

Her heart clenched with her lungs.

She rubbed the lotion into the smooth skin. Her heart unclenched and began to pound.

Up to his neck her hands worked, over the shoulder blades, down the spine, around the sides. By the time she reached the waistband of his swim shorts her lack of breath was no longer deliberate and her lips were tingling as she fought their yearning to press a kiss right into the centre of this sculpted masterpiece.

She had to physically force herself to step back, and when he turned and caught her eye, every organ in her body made a double flip.

'My turn,' he said, a slow, sensual smile forming.

'I...' The urge to lie and say she'd already screened her back was almost stronger than any future potential melanoma threat.

The sense of danger was stronger than ever.

She turned around.

Saying a prayer for luck, she forced air into her lungs and untied her sarong. It floated to her feet.

She heard him take a sharp intake of breath.

Her refilled lungs expelled in a whoosh the moment his fingers made contact with her skin.

Sensation shivered through her, deepening as his fingers slowly caressed the lotion over her back. When they dipped under the thin string holding her excuse of a bikini together, a wild fantasy sprang into her mind of him untying the knot and cupping her aching breasts...

She didn't even know breasts *could* ache. She didn't have to look down to know her nipples had puckered. She couldn't look down even if she wanted. It was taking everything she had to keep her gaze fixed ahead and to stop her legs from collapsing beneath her.

His fingers skimmed the top of her bikini bottoms. This time she could do nothing to stop the betraying quiver of her body.

Too much sun.

But this was okay! The thought punched through. This was okay. Better than okay. Wasn't she supposed to be leading Gianni on? Holding his interest in the only way a woman could because all he cared about when it came to women was the superficiality of their appearance and what he could get out of them in the bedroom.

She just had to keep hold of herself and not let her sun-addled brain trick her needy virgin body into believing it could possibly be attracted to one of the men directly responsible for the loss of everything she'd ever held dear. Her body was so starved it would likely react in the same way to any man!

His hands clasped her biceps. He was going to press himself against her.

Without warning to either him or herself, Issy stepped out of his hold, kicked her sandals off and, only just remembering to throw a cheeky grin over her shoulder, ran to the pool and jumped into the cool water.

Gianni didn't hesitate to follow her.

Dio, there was something about Issy's skin he reacted to, from her touch on him to his touch on her, infecting the whole of him, soaking him in erotic awareness.

By the time he dived into the pool, she'd swum to the far end, treading water as she faced him.

Half a dozen long strokes and he reached her.

Although she met his stare with that fantastic insouciance, she was trembling.

He closed the gap, gripping the walls of the pool on either side of her slender body, trapping her, and drank in her beauty.

She was ravishing. The most beautiful con woman to roam the earth. And the sexiest.

Thrums of desire beat heavily in him.

From the darkness in her pulsing eyes and the unsteadiness of her breaths, Issy was feeling it too.

It was time to up the ante.

Let the pleasure commence.

He sank his mouth into the softness of her lips in a full-bodied charged kiss of attrition. *Dio*, she tasted of champagne with added heat, a taste that roused his already electrified body, and he wrapped his arms around her and pulled her tight against him.

Her surrender was immediate. Her lips parted and in an instant her hands clasped the back of his head, fingers scratching through his hair and into his skull, and she was devouring him with the same hunger infusing him. With her small, high breasts crushed against his chest and her legs wrapped around his waist, her tongue duelling with his, Gianni's arousal was as thick and heavy as he had ever known it, jutting hard against her inner thigh.

Kissing Issy was like tasting honey from heaven and his excitement somehow managed to thicken and tighten even more to wonder if the rest of her tasted as if she'd been gift-wrapped by the king of the gods, Jupiter himself.

He would have to discover that another time because the moment he broke the kiss to drag his mouth over her cheek and to her neck, her fingers gripped his hair tightly and pulled his head back.

Her eyes were drugged with desire. He knew his eyes reflected the same.

She swallowed, then sucked in a breath. And then she released her grip on his hair, placed her hands to his chest and, with a giggle, pushed him back. 'Not so fast, big boy.'

He snapped his teeth at her. 'I can do slow.' Then he licked the lobe of her delicate ear and huskily added, 'I can do whatever you like.'

Hands laid lightly on his shoulders, she stretched her neck and, with a smile, gazed up at the clear azure sky. 'We have all the time in the world.'

Cupping her chin, he pressed a feather-kiss to her lips. 'All the time we need,' he whispered.

The drugged daze came back into her eyes but she blinked it away, then looked over his shoulder at something that had caught her eye and brightly said. 'Looks like lunch is ready. Come on, let's eat.'

Gianni stepped aside to release her. 'Give me a minute and I'll join you.'

Her pretty eyebrows drew in.

He grinned ruefully and dropped his stare to below the waterline. 'I need to cool off for a minute. I don't want to frighten the crew.'

She followed his gaze. A bright stain of colour crawled over her cheeks as understanding sank in, and it took her longer than normal to compose herself. 'Okay, probably best you stay here a while. Cold beer?'

'That would be great.'

She hauled herself out of the pool.

He didn't think he was imagining the slight stagger in her walk back to the lounging area.

Dio, her body…

No more focusing on that hot body, he scolded himself even as he internally sighed with disappointment when she wrapped a towel around it. Not while arousal still had its tentacles in him.

Maybe he should get Issy to bring the cold beer over and pour it down his swim shorts.

The staff were busy setting out plates and glasses on the deck's dining table. Issy had just finished retying her hair when she suddenly snatched her phone up and read whatever had just pinged into it. She was still reading when one of the crew approached her. She put her phone back on the table, nodded at whatever the crewman said, then indicated she would be two minutes to Gianni, and disappeared inside.

Gianni had never swum so fast in his life. He streaked through the water, hauled himself out and strode quickly to the table their stuff was on. Pressing his hand onto a towel a crew member had left for him, he grabbed Issy's phone.

'Tell me when she's on her way back,' he ordered the nearest crew member as he removed his own phone and top-of-the-range cloning device from the back pocket of the canvas shorts he'd left slung over a chair. In moments, he'd copied all the data from her phone onto his.

Carefully placing Issy's phone back where he'd found it, he dried himself off, removed his swim shorts, wrapped a dry towel around his waist, took a seat at the dining table and drank thirstily from the bottle of cold beer placed before him. Then, with a huge grin of satisfaction that came from knowing he'd upped the stakes in this game of chance in his favour, he swiped the screen of his phone for the first look at his bounty. Issy's screen saver appeared.

The grin died as his heart thumped then nose-dived in recognition.

He blinked, then blinked again, certain he must be seeing things.

The image of two young women, faces pressed together, smiling for the camera, remained.

The pulse at the side of his jaw throbbing, head pounding as he tried to make sense of something that absolutely did not make sense, he went into her messages.

The last of his euphoria died at the exact same moment his screen faded into nothing. Cloning Issy's phone had drained his battery.

But he'd seen enough.

This was no hustle.

This was a deliberate, targeted attack.

CHAPTER FOUR

Issy TOUCHED UP her lip gloss with a shaking hand. She needed to touch up her eyeliner but was too scared of stabbing herself in the eye to dare.

The lip gloss dropped from her hand and clattered in the sink. She clutched her flushed cheeks and gazed at her reflection. Her eyes had a fevered brightness to them. It was nothing to what was going on inside her.

Her heart was a pulsating mess, her limbs weak, her stomach as tight a knot as she'd ever known it. Between her legs…

She squeezed her eyes shut and tried to fill her lungs.

Okay, so she wasn't immune to Gianni's animal magnetism. No point in denying it. The main thing to remember was that she'd come to her senses before the situation had got even close to getting out of hand.

The situation that entailed Gianni turning her into flames.

What did flames do? They burned the object into ashes.

She'd kept control of the situation. She'd dealt with it.

But, heaven help her, her body still felt scorched in all the places they'd bound themselves so tightly together.

She could still feel his mouth devouring hers.

As part of all her preparation for this, she should have found some men to practice kissing with. Maybe then she'd have developed some immunity to the act and wouldn't have turned into a molten flame for him.

A careful swipe of bronzer against her cheeks and a fresh sarong around her, and she was ready to face him again. As ready as she'd ever be.

She found Gianni at the dining table, leaned back in his seat, casually drinking lager from a bottle so cold rivulets of condensation dripped down it. Not until he rose to his feet did she realise he had a towel wrapped around his waist. A quick dart of her eyes to where they'd been sitting found his swim shorts drying on the back of a chair. His canvas shorts were where he'd left them earlier.

A pulse throbbed between her legs. Beneath that towel, Gianni was naked.

'Everything okay?' he asked.

She nodded and smiled brightly. 'Just needed to freshen up. I hope you're hungry—Chef's made us a feast.'

His gaze held hers then drifted slowly down her bikini-clad body. 'I'm ravenous.'

Their first course was a fire roasted tomato soup Issy had loved since she was a little girl but had never been able to re-create for herself. The French chef must have sought an authentic Italian recipe for it because it was even better than she'd tasted as a child.

'Don't you eat bread?' Gianni asked, nodding at the freshly made bread roll she'd left on her side plate.

She shook her head and offered it to him, then tried not to salivate when he ripped it in two and slathered each piece with butter.

Not long, she consoled herself. Not long until she could bury her face in an ocean of carbs and not care that they all landed straight on her hips. She could heap a spoonful of sugar into her coffee *and* a dollop of cream if she wanted. She could buy herself a huge bar of hazelnut chocolate and eat it all in one sitting.

She'd been hungry for two whole years. She could wait a few days more. She would celebrate Gianni and his equally abhorrent cousin's destruction by indulging herself in all the delicious foods and treats she'd had to deny herself to maintain the stick insect look.

For their second course she'd selected fresh tuna, pan-fried in Japanese spices and served on a bed of couscous with roasted peppers. Fresh tuna was an expensive treat she could never normally afford under the strict budget Issy and Amelia imposed on themselves, and as it was healthy and her portion small, she ate the lot, then made sure to drink a whole glass of water to fill her up.

Dessert was freshly made strawberry ice cream on a chocolate crumb base but, as divine as it tasted, she allowed herself only a couple of small spoonsful before pushing the bowl to one side.

'Are there no foods you enjoy so much that you allow yourself to gorge?' Gianni asked, watching her closely. Issy's return to deck meant he'd had to compose himself quickly. Years of being able to adopt a poker face in stressful moments, dating back to a time when he didn't even know what a poker face was, just knew he didn't want to give his father the satisfaction of seeing fear in his eyes, meant his outward composure was no effort at all.

What was occurring beneath his skin was a whole different matter.

He felt like he'd been sucker-punched.

The lying, conniving temptress shook her head in answer.

Mio Dio, even Issy's slender frame was a lie.

Her screen saver kept playing in his mind's eye. He'd recognised the other woman before he'd recognised Issy. Well, what person wouldn't struggle to recognise the slender blonde picking at her food before him with the plump dark-chestnut-haired woman in the photo? The chestnut-haired woman, her face pressed against the other woman's, had gripped tightly to a huge ice cream sundae, as if afraid someone would snatch it away from her if she let go of it even for a photograph. Only the dark blue eyes had revealed her to be the lying, conniving temptress before him.

The broker must have lied to him about her name because the woman nibbling on a piece of lettuce was not Isabelle Clements. She was Isabelle Seymore. Daughter of the bastard who'd ripped off the Rossi cousins by selling them land it was impossible to build on and bribing the very people whose due diligence should have picked up that fact. Their first business deal still left a bitter taste on Gianni's tongue that even the revenge they'd taken on the man once they'd rebuilt themselves and conducted a hostile takeover of his company hadn't lessened.

Like father like daughter. Or, as he should say, like daughters. Plural. Because there were two Seymore sisters. And the other sister, the woman he'd instantly recognised in Issy's screen saver, was in a far more dangerous position to inflict lasting harm on the Rossi cousins.

Amelia Seymore. *Dio*, how long had she worked for them? Had to be two years. She was a good, diligent worker, the type who always arrived early, got her head down and got on with the job. No fuss. The kind of worker Gianni often wished others would be more like.

It had never crossed his mind that she was the daughter of the corrupt bastard who'd taken advantage of them in their first business deal. Not even her surname had given him pause for thought. Seymore was a reasonably common surname, and besides, who would be so blatant as to set up camp in the enemy's quarters under her real name?

Amelia Seymore, that's who.

Damn his phone for dying on him. He needed to warn Alessandro. He'd managed to get one of the crew to take it inside and charge it for him before Issy came back on deck, and it was taking all his willpower to keep his backside rooted to his chair and not storm inside to use it. To not unleash the full force of his fury on the conniving hussy actively seeking to destroy him.

He needed to keep his head. Give nothing away. Keep playing the game.

He took another drink of his second beer and contemplated Issy some more. There were many things he needed to do to shore up his defences, and warning his cousin was only one of them. From what he'd gleaned skimming her messages, the sisters were conducting a two-pronged attack, Amelia targeting the company, Issy tasked with keeping Gianni distracted until her sister's mission was complete. That mission revolved around the Aurora project for which she was the project manager.

Rossi Industries were on the cusp of making a creative partnership deal that would shake the property development world and send the cousins' already incredible wealth into the stratosphere. Today's leadership team meeting would be the decider on which company they partnered with. Gianni had already vetted it. He'd gone through every document with a fine-tooth comb. Nothing had jumped out at him. No warning flags about either of the final two short-listed companies. Nothing. He'd flown to the Caribbean content to leave the final decision on this to Alessandro knowing he would nip any trouble in the bud if it came to it. Whichever company they went with, they would be onto a guaranteed winner. Or so he'd believed.

What had he missed? He must have missed something.

Dammit!

He drained his bottle and reminded himself that whatever the outcome of the meeting, nothing would be signed today. He had time in that regard.

Issy didn't know he'd discovered her true identity.

He would make sure to keep it that way until they reached St Lovells, which was two days' sailing away from Barbados. Once on St Lovells, Issy would be powerless. St Lovells would be her kryptonite.

He needed to get rid of her phone. If he'd known when he cloned it the power it held, he'd have thrown it overboard or accidentally dropped it in the pool. It was seeing the two messages between Issy and her sister that had stopped his brain functioning as it should. The realisation that this was no mere hustle.

It was the message Amelia had sent to her sister two weeks ago that really churned his stomach.

They're corrupt. I have proof.

Churned it far more than the one written minutes after their meeting in London.

It worked! Hook, line and sinker.

What proof of corruption? Gianni and Alessandro were united in their demand their business be run straight down the line. They did not bribe. They did not lie. They did not cut corners. Their bastard fathers were the role models they used to work against and ensure everything they did was the opposite of how they would do it. Thomas Seymore's corrupt actions had only reinforced that ethos. Never mind the destructive fall-out such an accusation would bring, they'd been on the receiving end of malpractice and would never put anyone else through the same.

Any interrogation had to wait until they docked at St Lovells. Until then, he would take a leaf out of Issy's book and unleash the full force of his magnetism on her. Because that was the one big advantage he had—he knew damn well that for all her heinous plotting, Isabelle Seymore wanted him. He would play on that desire without mercy.

She didn't deserve his mercy.

He cast his gaze on her melting bowl of ice cream. 'May I?'

She lifted the bowl to him. 'Be my guest.'

'Grazie.'

'Prego.'

'You speak my language?'

There was a slight hesitation. 'Some.'

'I should have guessed seeing as you've given this beautiful vessel an Italian name.' Dipping his spoon into the ice cream, he lifted it to his mouth and added in Italian, 'I always think the best place to serve ice cream is on the naked body...and the best way to eat it is with my tongue.'

The dark stain of colour that flushed over her told him she'd understood him perfectly. The way she adjusted herself in her seat told him the image he'd evoked in her mind had infused into her body.

Smiling, he popped the spoon into his mouth.

Issy had to cross her legs tightly to stop herself from overtly squirming. But the bastard knew. She could see it in his eyes. He knew she'd understood his seductively delivered words and the effect they were having on her.

His command of the English language was so good it was easy to forget when speaking to him that Gianni was Italian. Hearing that deep, sensuous voice in his mother tongue...

It landed like a caress that penetrated deep into her core. His words had only added to the effect, and scrambled her brain to stop any quip forming.

Quite honestly, she needed to throw herself back into the pool to cool down.

God, she hoped the meeting in London was going to plan. Hoped the signing of the contracts was sped up and that it would all be wrapped up in a matter of days as Amelia expected and didn't drag on, because sitting there with Gianni's divinely masculine torso and heaven-sent face in her eye-line, the aftermath of the crush of their bodies still zinging through her skin and the mark of his mouth still on her lips...

This was hell.

Somehow she had to find a way to keep him distracted without compromising herself any further because she couldn't do this. It was too dangerous. Her awareness of Gianni was going through the roof. It was torture to even look him in the eye.

But look him in the eye she must, and she put her elbow on the table and rested her chin on her hand to murmur, 'We seem to be in a quiet stretch of water. How about I get the captain to anchor and we can get the slide out or take the Jet Skis for a spin?'

His eyes gave the sensuous glitter that melted her pelvis. '*Bella*, I've been fantasising about your slide since you first mentioned it.'

* * *

Issy contemplated the slide the crew had just finished inflating. Attached to the top sun deck and sweeping straight into the sea, it reminded her of a taller, narrow version of an airplane's safety slide. It wasn't just the slide that had been inflated. Next to where it jutted into the sea bobbed a giant square inflatable that could easily fit ten people on it. That too had been attached to the yacht.

She contemplated it because she wasn't the strongest of swimmers. She'd spent her childhood summers in and out of their Italian holiday home's swimming pool, but that had been a long time ago and, until that day, she hadn't been in a pool since. Even back then she'd never been interested in swimming itself, more interested in splashing around and trying to get a rise out of her sister by hurling beach balls at her head. Also, that had been a pool, with a definable bottom. She didn't dare ask the captain how deep the passage of water they'd anchored in was.

'Ready?' Gianni asked with that devilish grin of his.

Reminding herself that she was supposed to be a fearless society party girl, Issy grinned back. 'Race you to the top.'

She was off before she'd finished making her challenge, already darting up the steps to the next deck before Gianni realised what she was doing.

One good thing about working so hard on sculpting her body in recent years was that it had made her fit. Hungry, yes, but definitely fit. Also, it had made her quick on her feet, and she'd skipped up the first set of steps before Gianni even reached them. Laughing over her shoulder, she raced up the second set to the next deck, easily maintaining her lead, maintaining it too as she whipped up the third and final set… But no sooner had she put her foot on the top deck than a strong arm wrapped around her waist and lifted her in the air.

Legs flailing, she screamed, half in laughter and half in fright. For such a big man, she hadn't heard him closing in on her. He must have been holding himself back.

Dear God, she'd known Gianni was strong but he carried her near the top of the slide as if she weighed nothing, and when he put her down and twisted her round to face him, the size difference between them, even more prominent as she was barefoot, hit her starkly for the first time.

This man could break her in two with no effort whatsoever.

The sense of danger crept its way back through her but even as she tried to decipher it, she knew it was nothing to do with his size, that he would never use his physicality to hurt her.

He gazed down at her, blinked and shook his head. 'You're tiny.'

Uh-oh, she could feel a burn spread across her face. Gianni liked his women tall and leggy. In all her research she'd never learned of a lover who stood under five foot seven.

He placed his fingers under her chin and bowed his head. 'You carry yourself so tall but you're *tiny*.'

Impulsively, she pressed a finger to his lips. 'Don't tell anyone,' she said in a mock whisper. 'It's a secret.'

He stared at her for another beat and then burst into a roar of laughter. Issy couldn't help it. The sound was so infectious that laughter escaped her own lips, and when he put his hands to her sides and lifted her into the air so her face rose above his and her hair, which she'd set free, hung down like a waterfall, the compulsion to kiss him was so strong that it took everything she had to resist.

But resist she must. Even if her body did feel like it was on fire. 'Can you put me down please?'

His shoulders rose slowly before he acquiesced. But there was no time for her to make a break for distance. No sooner did her feet touch the deck than he pressed a hand into the small of her back and wiped a strand of hair off her face. 'You're beautiful.'

'Even though I'm short one end?' she quipped, a quip she was thankful and proud of making because those two words made her feel all fuzzy...but not as fuzzy as the look in his eyes did.

Heaven help her, everything about this man made her feel fuzzy.

Did she fancy him?

His gleaming sensuality burned through her. 'Small but perfectly formed.'

A sharp pang sliced through her chest and she had to work doubly hard not to show it.

It shouldn't even bother her! After all, wasn't this proof that all the money she and Amelia had scrimped and saved for over the years so Issy could pull off Gianni's version of perfection had worked? She should be glad they hadn't needed to invest in a stretching machine for her, not have her heart twist at the knowledge that he wouldn't look twice at the real Issy and certainly wouldn't consider her perfect.

Who *cared* what he thought? Not her. Once the deal in London was signed, sealed and delivered, she would disappear from his life and never see him again.

For the first time, Gianni saw the brightness Issy had maintained all this time in her eyes dim. In seconds she'd blinked it back to brightness, but he'd seen it and he wondered what had caused it, and then wondered why the hell he cared for the cause.

Aware of arousal strengthening in him, he reluctantly slipped his arm away from her, took a step back and indicated the slide. 'Ladies first.'

She smiled sweetly. 'Age before beauty.'

He sniggered. She might be a lying, conniving temptress set on his destruction but she amused him. It had been a long time since he'd enjoyed a woman's company—anyone's company, come to that—so much, and when he cupped her cheeks and planted a hard, passionate kiss to her mouth, it was sheer impulse driving him with nothing calculated behind it.

Dio, she tasted so good.

'Seeing as I am here at your whim, ready to comply with your every wish, I will do the honours.' And with that, he climbed the three steps to the top of the slide, sat himself down and then let himself fall.

Issy peered over the balustrade and watched the enormous splash made when he landed. A knot of anxiety formed when he didn't immediately surface but it barely had time to root when his dark head suddenly appeared and, after wiping water from his eyes, his grinning face tilted up to hers.

Okay. Now it was her turn.

She could do this. To back out would only make him suspicious, and she couldn't afford that.

She remembered a time when a day at a splash park had been the height of fun, and charging down water slides of all shapes and sizes the biggest thrill of her life.

But those slides all landed in pools of water with a definable bottom and a host of lifeguards overlooking.

Stop being a wimp!

Resolved not to think about what she was about to do, she skipped up the three steps, waved at Gianni treading water a safe distance from the landing zone, plonked her bottom down and let go.

It felt exactly like what she imagined it would feel to free-fall. It was also much quicker than she'd anticipated, the water pouring down the slide as a lubricant hurtling her to the upward curving base so quickly she had no time to prepare or brace herself for the landing. Into the air she flew before slamming into the sea with a scream. Salt water shot up her nose and into her open mouth as she submerged into the depths.

CHAPTER FIVE

GIANNI'S AMUSEMENT AT the spectacularly ungraceful way Issy flipped in the air before crashing into the water vanished when she resurfaced in a panic of flailing arms. He didn't hesitate to streak through the water to her.

The moment he hooked an arm around her waist to stabilise her, she flung her arms around his neck and clung like a limpet to him.

'Hey, take it easy,' he chided when there was a danger she would drag him under. 'I've got you. Relax.'

Blonde hair splattered all over her face, dark blue eyes fixed onto his. She loosened her hold the tiniest fraction.

'Okay?' he asked.

Her lips pulled in before she nodded.

'Good.' Treading water for them both, he kissed her lightly. 'Can you swim to the inflatable?'

Still holding tightly to him, she turned her head to gauge the distance. It was only ten metres or so from where they were but he guessed from the look in her eyes that it could be ten miles as far as she was concerned.

'Hold on to my back,' he said. 'I'll swim us to it.'

Without losing her touch on his body, she twisted around him until she was gripping on to his back like a baby orangutan clinging to its mother.

'As great as it feels to have your legs wrapped around me like this, you need to loosen up a bit if I'm going to be able to swim,' he told her drily. 'Trust the water's buoyancy and trust me. I've got you.'

Issy's definition of loosening up differed greatly to Gianni's, but at least she relaxed her hold enough for him to move his arms semi-freely.

Life took the strangest of turns he thought as he made his way steadily to the inflatable. Issy Seymore was here to destroy him and now she was holding on to him as if he were her personal life raft. If this had occurred two hours ago when he'd first learned her real identity, he'd have been tempted to let her suffer and flail her own way there. He almost grunted aloud to know this thought was a lie. He planned to make Issy Seymore suffer for the hell she intended to unleash on him but that didn't extend to physical harm.

Once they reached the giant inflatable, he helped her crawl onto it then hauled himself up beside her.

She'd laid herself on her back, her gaze fixed to the sky, breathing heavily.

Stretching himself out on his side beside her, he traced a finger along a high cheekbone. 'Better now?'

Her eyes closed before she turned onto her side to

face him and locked on to his stare. 'Thank you for rescuing me.'

'My pleasure,' he murmured.

'Your pleasure? I almost drowned you.'

'*Bella*, you're half my size. You couldn't have drowned me if you'd tried.' Except maybe with her eyes. Gazing into them was like gazing into a deep, hypnotising pool. *Dio*, even half drowned, and with most of her make-up washed away apart from where her mascara had smeared beneath her eyes, she was ravishing. Desire stirred within him and he inched his face closer to hers and splayed a hand on her hip. Her drying skin felt impossibly smooth and soft to his touch.

But he could have drowned her, Issy realised, shivering at the thought even as tendrils of awareness unfurled inside her at his touch and the closeness of their bodies. It would have taken no effort on Gianni's part at all. He could have simply watched her splash around until exhaustion got the better of her. If he knew who she really was he'd probably have helped her drown.

Oh, what a plonker she'd made of herself, and it made her cheeks burn to think of how she'd banged on about 'her' yacht's slide, and then how, at the first go on it, she'd panicked at the speed she'd hurtled down it and flailed like a madwoman when she landed.

The burn deepened to recall how her fear had left her the moment Gianni had taken hold of her. She hadn't clung so tightly to him out of fear of drowning but because her body had instinctively equated Gianni, the man who'd destroyed her life, with safety. The irony was enough to make her splutter a laugh even as an ache deep inside her grew at the wish to wind her arms around him again.

'What's so funny?' he asked, nudging close enough for the tips of their noses to touch.

She plucked a plausible answer out of her scrambling brain; scrambling because it wasn't just their noses touching. The tips of her breasts had brushed against his chest and in an instant, the tendrils of awareness had turned into flames. She cleared her throat. 'I'm just thinking how undignified I must have looked when I landed in the water.'

Amusement played on the lips that had given her so much heady pleasure. 'It was one of those moments where you wish for a video camera.'

Her splutter turned into a giggle. As much as she despised him, there was a dry wit about Gianni that tickled her, and she hated him even more for it. She loathed everything about him. Most especially loathed that he was the sexiest man to roam the earth and that she was practically melting with anticipation for his hand to move from her hip and explore the contours of her body properly.

God help her, she was aching for his touch.

God help her, she *did* fancy him. There was no other explanation for it. She desired the devil.

'I can't believe I panicked like that,' she bluffed, scrambling even more valiantly for clarity in her thoughts. She couldn't let her body's treacherous responses get the better of her, not when so much was at stake. Having sold herself as a party girl and water sports lover, she couldn't have Gianni think she'd panicked because she hated being out of her depth in water. That would contradict everything she'd purported to be.

His smile was lazy and totally belied the heat pulsing from his eyes. 'These things happen. No harm done.'

But she feared harm had been done. To her. Because the warmth of his breath brushing over her mouth and his thumb gently making circles on her hip was filling her with even more of those thrilling flames. An ache had formed deep inside her, the urge to press her pelvis forwards so that her groin locked with his almost unbearable in its intensity.

'Have you saved many hapless women's lives before?' she asked, striving for a form of nonchalant brightness in her tone but succeeding only in sounding breathless.

'You're the only one I've succeeded with,' Gianni replied, and as his fingers tightened their grip on Issy's delectable hip, his thoughts strayed to his mother. He'd wanted to save her and his aunt from their bastard husbands. Alessandro had too. When their fathers' mother, the matriarch of their family, died, the buffer to their cruelty had gone. Neither Gianni nor his cousin had appreciated how much their *nonna*'s presence at their farmhouse had kept a curb on her sons' malice. Her death unleashed it to a terrifying degree. How he'd longed to have superhero powers—he'd believed back then, when he was eight, that it needed a superhero to stop his father using his fists against himself and his mother—and the money to whisk them off some-where safe. Turned out his mama didn't need saving. She'd saved herself. When Gianni was nine years old, he'd woken one morning to find her gone. He'd never seen her again.

Naturally, it had been a distressing time for a young boy, but he'd got over it. By the time he was twelve, Gianni and Alessandro had dreamed up their plan to leave. A cast-iron dream left little room for the ado-lescent Gianni to think about his mother or deal with the churn of anguish as to how she could have left him.

Strangely, he hadn't allowed himself to remember that long-ago anguish for so long that to suddenly think about it now was disconcerting. Emotional pain was something he'd never allowed himself to feel again. In this whole world he loved and trusted Alessandro, and that was it. This beautiful conniving woman gaz-ing at him with eyes ablaze with desire was poison. If she had her way, she could destroy him as effec-tively as his mother had once done. But not emotion-ally. When it came to his heart, she couldn't touch him. No one could.

Issy was poison…but she was a hot poison. Her poi-sonous intentions couldn't quell the attraction smoul-dering thickly between them. Her poisonous intentions only added piquancy to it. Gianni wanted to taste her venomous lips again and, when her fingers finally closed around his hips and the tips dug through the material of his shorts, his desire ran free to imagine losing himself in all her beautiful toxicity.

'We'll have to get you a pair of red lifeguard shorts

and one of those banana board things,' she murmured, her mouth so close to his that the scent of her sweetly toxic breath filled his senses.

There was venom in her breath for sure, a potent drug designed to bewitch and enthral and thicken the desire already rampaging through him. What she didn't know was that her poison could only work on a base level with him. He didn't deny that on a base level it was stronger than any other desire he'd experienced, infecting him right through to his pores, coming close to making him tremble with its strength. Dragging his hand around her back, he clasped her bottom and pulled her flush against him, letting her feel the strength of his excitement. 'Banana board things?'

She hitched a breath before answering. Her eyes had become glazed and when she spoke, there was a breathless quality to her voice. 'You know, those things lifeguards carry under their arms when they're running to save someone from drowning.'

He brushed his mouth against her toxically sweet lips. 'Do you mean a float?'

Her beautiful face flush with colour, she made a noise through her nose he supposed was meant to be a laugh and pressed her breasts tighter against his chest. 'Probably. I'll send you one for your birthday.'

He squeezed her bottom and ground himself harder against her, loving the barely perceptible shock that quivered through her and the pressure of her fingers on his hips. 'What if I need to save your life again before my birthday?'

Her eyes were now so dark and drugged with desire

he could see the fight she was waging to keep control of herself. There was barely any coherence in her voice, but somehow she managed to keep the banter going. 'You'll just have to use your superhero powers again.'

'I'm no superhero, *bella*. Just a man.' A man with a deep hunger for another taste of Issy's poisonous lips. Finally fusing his mouth to hers, Gianni rolled on top of her and sank into the heady pleasure of her mouth.

Oh, God, didn't she know how much of a man he was? Issy thought wildly as red-hot lava pumped through her veins. The feelings Gianni elicited in her were so out of this world, a craven need that his touch and ravenous mouth only fed, that she gave no thought to resisting. With his weight on her, covering her, sub-suming her, the essence of herself slipped out of her grasp and she stepped into the flames of desire.

His kisses were hard and demanding, a devouring of mouths and tongues, a sensory whirl that had her press her screaming, sensitised skin tightly against every inch of him that she could. Dragging her fingers over Gianni's smooth, muscular back, she revelled in the groans he made at her touch and kissed him even harder, only breaking her mouth from his to gasp at the shock that thrilled through her when the weight and length of his excitement jutted through his swim shorts and jabbed against the scrap of material covering her most intimate parts. It was a thrill that burned deep in the heart of her and instinctively, she wrapped her legs tight around his waist and raised her hips.

She didn't know if the rocking motion was all them or if the swell of the water beneath the inflatable they were locked in each other's arms on was the cause and she didn't care. A burning coil had wound itself tightly in her core and was throbbing with a desperate need for relief, and she clung even tighter, kissing him even harder as the length of his thick hardness thrust against her swollen nub and...

The coil sprang free without warning. One minute she was rocking against him, caught up in the most heavenly thrills she'd ever experienced in her life; the next she shattered, and even as the unexpected explosions of her very first climax throbbed and raged through her, still she clung to Gianni, burying her face in his neck, desperate to keep the connection between them and draw out this most incredible moment of her life.

It was only when the spasms subsided and Issy realised Gianni had stilled that she came back to earth with a sharp bump. In an instant, the crest of the most glorious experience she'd ever ridden was over and sanity crashed into her like a bucket of ice being tipped over her head.

Oh, God, what had just happened?

She squeezed her eyes shut and wished for a hole to open in the inflatable and to sink beneath the surface and never come back up again.

This was terrible. Horrendous.

She tried to breathe. Tried to think. Then she tried not to think because even as the last thrills limped through her, her head was swimming with the fact that she'd just come completely undone and behaved in the most shocking, wanton, shameful fashion. And for *him*.

And all in her bikini. He hadn't even needed to touch her there.

The weight crushing her slowly lifted, but only the physical weight. She could feel Gianni staring at her. What must he think of her? She shouldn't care what he thought of her. She *didn't* care. She didn't.

She needed to bluff her way out of this, and as she realised this, the path of least humiliation opened to her. She just had to get back into character. It was beyond belief that any of his previous lovers had cared two hoots about seeming wanton to him. Wanton was what Gianni wanted!

As humiliating as her responses to him were, she needed to think of them in a positive light. Most importantly though, she must take more care than ever not to let desire for him overtake her sanity again. Use this as a warning to keep her internal guard up.

Gianni, struggling to find his breath, studied Issy's flushed face intently. His head was reeling from what had just occurred between them. Their kiss in the pool had blown his mind. This had come close to blowing his head off his shoulders. And hardly anything had happened. He was still to taste anything but her mouth.

But never had he experienced such unbridled hunger before. *Dio*, the ache in his loins was like nothing he'd felt before. Her passion...

His loins were on fire. He ached so badly to smother her mouth again and continue what they'd started. The fusion of their mouths had sent an inferno raging through them, from simmer to scorching in an instant. When he'd sensed what was happening to her... It hadn't seemed possible.

But it had been real. Issy had climaxed. He guessed from the ragged sharpness of her breathing and the way her eyes were still screwed so tightly together that it had been as big a shock to her as it was to him.

Just as shocking was how close to the edge he'd come too.

What the hell was happening to him? He was thirty-two years old. He'd learned to control his bodily responses to beautiful women before the end of his adolescence. He took *pride* in his control so to know that a few beats longer with their groins locked together would have tipped him over the edge too was beyond his comprehension. Issy was beautiful and sexy but so were plenty of other women. He'd never come close to losing control like that before.

Finally, Issy's eyes opened. After a moment's hesitation, they locked on to his. Gianni's heart slammed hard against his ribs.

After another beat, a lazy smile formed on her beautiful face. 'I need a drink. Let's go back.'

Disbelief almost made him mute. 'That's all you have to say?'

'I'm thirsty.' Laughing, she pushed at his chest and rolled out from beneath him.

His mouth opened and he shook his head. This woman was unbelievable, and he shook his head again as he watched her grip one of the handles around the inflatable's edge and slip into the water.

'Are you coming?' she asked with a tilt of her head and a knowing smile.

He laughed through the pain in his loins. 'I wish.'

She gave the faintest of winks. 'I guess you'll just have to wish harder.'

Before he could think of an answer, she'd pushed herself away from the inflatable and swum the metre distance to the steps the crew had earlier lowered for them.

Warm though the sea was, Gianni's body was on such a high simmer that when he followed Issy's lead, it was like sinking into a cold bath. He welcomed it. God help him, he was as horny as a sex-mad teenager, and as he watched her step onto the deck, all he could think of was untying those scraps of material covering her most feminine parts and screwing her until neither of them could stand.

Issy had no idea how she kept her back straight and stopped her legs from collapsing, and when she looked over her shoulder as she padded over the deck and saw Gianni's head appear by the railing, the swelling in her heart was so painful and the weakness in her legs so strong that the truth that she was in over her head slapped her like a wet fish.

She needed to message Amelia and beg her to at least try and fast-track the signing of the contracts. Get them signed immediately. She couldn't play this game for much longer. She needed to get as far away from Gianni as she could. He was just too much. All the research in the world couldn't have prepared her for the reality of seducing a man into distraction when the man in question brought out feelings in her that had never existed before. *She* was the one being seduced here, by the devil himself.

Upping her pace, mentally composing the message she would send to her sister, she reached the table she'd left her stuff on and in seconds found herself close to tears. Her phone had gone.

CHAPTER SIX

'SOMETHING WRONG?' GIANNI asked casually as he reached for his towel. He could not fathom why Issy's obvious anxiety should make his heart twinge.

She shook her sarong out. 'I can't find my phone.'

Of course she couldn't. He'd instructed the crew to hide it in his cabin, the only space in the yacht kept locked and off-limits to Issy. She could have it back when this was all over.

'It can't have gone far,' he assured her. 'Where did you last have it?'

'Right here. I left it on this table.'

He looked at his watch. It was coming up to ten p.m. in London. The meeting on the Aurora project would have finished hours ago. He could not let what had happened between him and Issy distract him from what needed to be done. He'd got rid of her phone so she was unable to contact her sister. His priority now was to warn Alessandro.

'Ask your crew,' he said. 'Maybe one of them took it inside for you when they took mine in to charge or when they finished clearing lunch.'

She bit her lip and nodded. 'Good idea.'

'If they haven't got it, it might be worth checking your cabin in case one of the crew put it in there for you and forgot to tell you.'

She nodded again, and hurried inside, forgetting to sway her hips seductively in her distraction. For some reason, this too made his heart twinge.

Pushing away the strange feelings threading through him—he needed to work fast and concentrate—he indicated to Mara, the head of his crew, to bring his phone to him.

He switched it on and immediately called his cousin.

Alessandro's voice sounded down the crackly line. 'Gianni, how—?'

'Andro, listen, I don't have much time.'

'Okay, but what's the—?'

'Amelia Seymore,' he interrupted. 'She's Thomas Seymore's daughter.'

'*What?* I can't hear you properly.'

'Listen to me, Amelia Seymore is a traitor. She's been a spy this whole time. She's working with her sister to destroy us.'

'Amelia Seymore?' Alessandro's incredulity was clear.

'Yes! Seymore! The Aurora project is compromised. And listen, she claims to have found some kind of proof of corruption against us.'

'Did you say corruption? What corruption?'

'I don't know, but according to the messages I read, Amelia Seymore has found evidence of corruption by us. I'm in the Caribbean with her sister. I'll keep her out of the way here and stop her communicating with anyone and causing any more damage. Can you deal with Amelia? This needs to be nipped in the bud and damage limitation undertaken immediately.'

'Consider it done,' Alessandro said, his voice now low and dangerous.

Despite the bad reception, the message had got through, and a fraction of the tightness in Gianni's chest loosened. 'I may be out of reach for a while,' he said, 'but I'll try and get a message to you when I know what's going on.'

'Likewise. Speak soon, cousin.'

Gianni disconnected the call and took a deep breath of relief. His cousin was like a human missile when it came to taking down targets. Amelia Seymore stood no chance now she was in his sights. Whatever she and her sister had planned against them would fail.

But that still left Issy to deal with. She was an unknown quantity. The messages he'd read suggested her only job was to distract him while Amelia did the dirty work, but who knew what plans they'd concocted in the privacy of their home that had left no digital trace.

By the time she came back out on deck, now wearing a black vest with spaghetti straps over a black bikini and a pair of tiny denim shorts, her large shades once again covering much of her face, he knew the only safe thing to do was proceed with his own plan and get her to St Lovells. On the open sea at this time of year, there were too many other yachts about, too many ways for her to escape the *Palazzo delle Feste* and reach safety and communication with another vessel. There would be no escape for her from St Lovells. Not without his explicit agreement.

'Did you find your phone?' he asked as she approached him.

She shook her head. 'I have no idea what's happened to it.'

'It will turn up,' he assured her.

Flopping onto the sofa across from his, she tucked her legs under her bottom. 'I hope so.'

Unable to resist, he held his phone out. 'You can always use mine if you need it. It's fully charged.'

'Thank you but I don't know any of my contacts' numbers.' Her shoulders rose. 'I suppose it's the curse of the age we live in that we don't need to commit people's phone numbers to memory.'

'You mean you want to use your phone to make an actual phone call?' he asked in pretend horror, and was rewarded with a definite loosening of her taut frame and a snuffle of laughter.

'I know. Who'd have thought it, 'eh? Using a phone to call people on. Whatever next?'

'People using televisions to watch TV?'

'Now you're going too far.' The amusement on her face dimmed a little. She raised her face to the sky and sighed. 'When I was a little girl, my mum had one of those old-fashioned address books, you know the ones where you could write someone's name in it along with their address and phone number?'

'I am familiar with old-fashioned address books,' he said drily. His *nonna* had had one that had been crammed full of names, and random pieces of paper with scribbled numbers that used to fly onto the floor whenever the book was opened. 'Some people still use them.'

'Do you reckon? I used to laugh at Mum for keeping one and thought it hilarious that she could still recite her childhood phone number from memory. It just seemed so old-fashioned and unnecessary to me when everything could be stored on your phone. I know my phone will turn up and if it doesn't, I'll be able to buy another one and retrieve all my data, but I can just imagine my mum—as she was back then—laughing at me now for relying on technology when the old-fashioned way would have made it more likely I had it stored in my brain.'

'You say as she was back then… You mentioned before something about her being in rehab. If you don't mind me asking, what is she in rehab for?' He leaned back, managing to resist the temptation to fold his arms across his chest and stare at her like a headmaster waiting for a rule-breaking student to come up with a wild non-convincing lie to get them off the hook.

Slowly, Issy lowered her face and met Gianni's stare through the darkness of their respective shades. While she'd made her fruitless search for her phone and showered the sea salt off her skin, the space away from Gianni had been the space she needed to talk sense back into herself. She and Amelia had spent ten years working towards this point. She could not throw it away just because of a major case of hormone problems for the bastard she was so desperate to bring down. And one of those reasons she so desperately wanted to bring him down was because of her mother. Because one of the many consequences of Gianni destroying her life had been the loss of the mother who'd once cherished and adored her two daughters. Jane Seymore was alive only in the sense that her heart still pumped blood through her body. 'She has many issues. Drugs is the biggest one.'

'Your mother is a drug addict?'

Yes, you bastard. Because of you.

'She's not a junkie in the traditional sense that people think of drug addicts. She doesn't inject herself thank God but that's only because she has a needle phobia. It's mostly strong prescription stuff delivered to the comfort of her home—dealers nowadays have diversified into home delivery. Basically, she takes whatever she can get her hands on that stops her having to think or feel.' Anything that stopped her remembering all that she'd lost.

There was a flicker in his eyes and she suddenly had the sense that he was weighing up whether or not to believe her. 'How long has she been like this?'

'If you don't mind, I'd rather not spoil this beautiful day by talking about it.' Not with him, the cause of it all. Not when she was unlikely to be able to get through a conversation about it without breaking character and screaming and hurling anything she could get her hands on at him. It was hard enough maintaining the high-society character as things stood, what with all the awful, awful, *wonderful* feelings he'd let loose in her body. She'd deliberately seated herself on a separate sofa to him but the tempest happening inside her was as acute as if she'd curled herself on his lap. God help her, he didn't need to actually touch her for her to want him. All he had to do was look at her, and for the first time, she felt a pang of sympathy for all the women who'd fallen under his spell before her. She'd assumed for years that all they wanted of him was his money and the glamour of his lifestyle but as she was learning, there was far more to him than that. What chance had those women had? No wonder Gianni had a litany of broken hearts strewn in his wake.

After a long beat, he said, 'I respect that, but if you're worried about her not being able to contact you then we can get in touch with the rehab facility and give them my number to reach you on.'

Issy hated the pang that ripped through her chest and belly at this sincerely delivered offer. Her mother was in rehab because of him! She shook her head. 'It's fine. They can call my sister if there's a problem. It's Amelia I'm more concerned about not being able to reach me—I can't remember her phone number or email address off the top of my head.'

'Amelia is your sister?'

'Yes.' Mentally kicking herself for mentioning Amelia by name, Issy shifted in her seat and quickly changed the subject, moving the conversation along to the next phase of keeping Gianni distracted and preferably uncommunicable while Amelia made the final moves in the Seymore sisters' destruction of the Rossi cousins, casually saying, 'As we're too far from the nearest island to dock before night falls, I thought we could anchor at sea tonight.'

His eyes flickered at the change of subject before a slow smile spread across his far too gorgeous face. 'Is that an invitation for me to spend the night with you?'

'It's an invitation for you to spend the night on the yacht. Not necessarily with me.' Never, never, never. No matter how badly she burned for him.

A gleam formed. 'Playing hard to get?'

'Nothing good ever comes easy,' she riposted sweetly, thinking she didn't need to just play hard to get but needed to build a fortress of concrete to make herself immune to him.

He raised the short crystal glass filled with an amber liquid that she hadn't noticed him holding, probably because she was too mesmerised by his face. 'That's a truth I will gladly drink to.'

'So what do you say?' Issy asked after he'd taken a sip. She wished she had a drink. It was easier to play seductress with a prop in her hand.

'About me staying the night here?'

She nodded. If he said no then she'd move to plan B and order the captain to fake engine problems. 'All the cabins are made up.'

'As you just said we're too far from anywhere to dock tonight, that suggests I don't actually have a choice about staying on board,' he pointed out.

'You can always swim.'

His strong throat extended as he laughed. How she hated the way the sound of it rang like balm in her ears and hated the way it enlivened his face, amplifying his heartbreaking handsomeness. 'I'm a strong swimmer but as we've already determined, I'm no superhero.'

'You could steal one of the Jet Skis.' That would work. If she was lucky, he might fall off. But even as she thought that a nibble of panic chewed at her heart at the prospect of him falling into open waters without even a life jacket for safety, and she quickly scrubbed it from her mind.

He pretended to mull this over. 'Hmm… Escaping on a Jet Ski or spending the night with the most beautiful woman in the Caribbean… That's a hard choice.'

'Spending the night on board a *yacht* with, not necessarily in *bed* with,' she reiterated.

He sighed mockingly. 'It's the hope that always kills, but even so, that's hope enough for me.'

'You'll stay?'

The gleam in his eyes turned up a notch and lasered straight into her pelvis. 'Trust me, *bella*. I'm not going anywhere.'

'Nice cabin,' Gianni commented as he stepped through the door Issy had opened for him on the sleeping deck. He'd wondered which cabin she would put him in. He'd bet she'd been tempted to put him in the smallest. Not that any of the cabins were small by any reasonable judgement. Gianni loved to party and took his duties as host seriously. The last thing he wanted was for any of his guests to feel slighted by being given inferior accommodation. The irony that his first night on his new yacht would be spent in the third-best cabin— the master suite was locked and Issy had claimed the second-best for her own—did not escape him. Still, it was spacious and had a perfectly respectable king-size bed. Gianni usually slept in an emperor bed, but this would do for one night. He turned his gaze from the cabin to the woman hovering at the foot of the doorway.

'The en suite is filled with toiletries and there's robes in the wardrobe you can use,' she said. For once, she seemed to be avoiding his eye. She'd dodged the elevator that would have taken them to the deck, skipping up the stairs ahead of him and then heading straight to the cabin. He knew perfectly well Issy was doing her best to stay out of arm's reach of him and knew perfectly well why. When she'd set off on her mission to destroy him she hadn't factored that she would actually want him, that she wouldn't have to fake desire for him. It must be killing her. Great. Let her suffer, trapped in the web of her own making.

He had to give her kudos though for the slick way she'd engineered for him to spend the night and admire how she'd made promises that weren't promises at all. The promise of what could come…but only maybe.

Did she really think she could hold out against the scorching chemistry between them for the duration of however long she intended to entrap him for?

'I'm going to get ready for dinner,' she added. 'I'll see you in an hour.'

Before she could run away, he pulled his polo shirt off and dropped it on the floor. She hesitated, her gaze fluttering over his chest before rising to meet his stare.

Poor Issy. She had no idea how expressive her eyes were, how her desire rang out from them. If she knew, she'd wear her shades permanently.

He stepped over to her. Linking his fingers through

hers, he gently pulled her hands above her head and trapped her against the wall. Her breathing shortened. That delicious colour he was coming to get such a thrill at provoking stained her cheeks.

'Want to take a shower with me before you go?' he murmured.

Her throat moved and her chest rose before she managed to make her lips curve and huskily say, 'A generous offer but judging by the size of you, you'll hog all the water.'

'Oh, I can be generous, *bella*.' Dipping his mouth down to her neck, he traced his tongue over the delicate, toxically sweet skin, revelling at the quiver of her body in response. 'Before our time here is done, I'll prove just how generous a man I can be.'

'Your self-confidence is staggering,' she said, only the hitches in her voice betraying her nonchalance as a facade.

Dropping her hands, he dragged his fingers through her hair and down her neck until, for the very first time, he palmed a small, pert breast. A shock of electricity zinged through them both, so tangible he could swear he heard it crackle.

'*Dio*, you're sexy,' he muttered into her mouth before kissing her. His arousal, a semi-permanent state since their first kiss in the swimming pool, sprung back to full length at the first flicker of her tongue against his and when she cupped his head and her fingers dug through his hair to scrape against his skull, his intention of merely teasing her was completely forgotten as the heat she evoked in him unleashed in all its power, a surge of energy that burned from his loins to every crevice in his body.

The way Issy Seymore made him feel was more than a mere game. He'd never wanted anyone like he wanted her.

This time, though, Issy was the one to keep her head, suddenly pulling her mouth from his and pushing him away from her.

'I can't do this,' she croaked, breathing heavily.

'Do what?'

'This. Gianni...' Clearly flustered, she pressed a hand tightly against her heaving chest. 'I...'

'You what?' he encouraged. Would this be the moment Isabelle Seymore confessed? Or did the little minx have something else up her sleeve?

Her dark blue eyes gazed into his with something akin to desperation. 'I'm saving myself for marriage.'

As soon as the words left her mouth, Issy wished she could take them back. She had no idea where they had come from. Of course she wasn't saving herself for marriage—she wasn't a Victorian!

But she *was* frightened. Terrified. Terrified at how easily her body overrode her sanity when it came to Gianni. Terrified at how deeply she was coming to crave him. So while her words of marriage had dredged themselves from nowhere, there was a slight calming in the wild thumps of her heart to know they were the words to make the commitment-phobic Gianni Rossi back off.

Gazing into his shocked eyes, she determined that

when this was all over, she was going to find herself a boyfriend. She'd make Amelia get out there and find a boyfriend too. The Rossi cousins had stopped them living for long enough.

This craving for Gianni was all his fault. If Gianni and his hateful cousin hadn't ruined their lives then they would have continued developing like other teenage girls, getting boyfriends and partying, not trying desperately to save their father from himself and then trying to save their mother, and all the while working and working to reach this point where they could bring down the men who'd turned their lives into rubble. Gianni's actions all those years ago had stopped her forming the emotional and sexual attachments other twenty-three-year-old women took for granted. Something else to hate and blame him for.

Her loathing ratcheted up when his shock slowly dissipated and that hateful gleam flashed in his devil eyes. 'You're saving yourself for marriage, *bella*?'

Grinding her toes into her sandals, she jutted her chin. 'Yes. I'm sorry if that disappoints you.'

He shrugged with the nonchalance she kept aiming for, and, leaning his face closer to hers, folded his arms across his naked chest. How her fingers itched to swirl through the dark hair covering it. The bastard had probably taken his polo shirt off deliberately. She wished he'd put it back on.

'Why would I be disappointed? There are other ways to share pleasure.'

Oh, God, did he have to say *pleasure* so ruddy seductively? 'I just thought you might have expectations…expectations that I've admittedly fed…' There was no getting around that. She'd practically promised herself to him. Feeling more confident, she continued. 'I am very much attracted to you, Gianni…' She managed to flash a grin. '…as you've probably noticed.'

'I'm pretty damned hot for you too.'

'And I know I've led you on but it's only because I fancied you from the moment I met you and I thought you could be the one I dropped my morals for, but they're too strong. I can't give myself to you without a ring on my finger. I'm sorry.'

His mouth curved and his forehead creased in understanding. 'No need to apologise. If you have morals then you must stick by then.'

'I'm so glad you understand.'

'I understand perfectly. You'll only have sex with me if I marry you?'

'Yes.'

'Then I accept.'

'Accept what?'

'Your proposal.'

'I beg your pardon?'

'Your proposal of marriage.' He stepped forwards and pressed her back against the wall, bringing his face so close to hers that she could practically feel the glitter burning from his eyes in her retinas. 'I accept.'

CHAPTER SEVEN

THE MIXTURE OF emotions that flittered over Issy's beautiful face filled Gianni with amusement. He'd caught her out. Anticipation for what she would do now filled him.

'You cannot be serious,' she said incredulously. 'You want to marry me just so you can sleep with me?'

'Why not? We're having fun, just as you promised, aren't we? What could be more fun than getting married?' He cupped her breast. *Dio*, it felt so good against the palm of his hand. He'd be tempted to marry her for real just to feel it naked against him. 'Come on, Issy,' he goaded, moving his hand from her breast to thread his fingers through her hair and clasp the back of her head, 'what is life for but taking risks, and we're both risk takers. Let's get married and spend the rest of our time on the Caribbean having wild sex.'

He was playing her, Issy knew, even as a thrill of need pulsed low in her pelvis at the unbidden thought of locking herself away with Gianni and acting out every depraved need that had exploded for him. This was nothing but a Gianni tactic to get her into bed. Pretend to want to marry her so that she'd drop her bikini bottoms for him. The man must be a bigger sex-mad cad than she'd supposed.

Knowing this was all just a game made it easier to deal with. She didn't even have to fake her laughter at the absurdity of the swerve to their conversation. 'I'd be up for that but I'm afraid I'd need a ring on my finger before having the wild sex you promise, so unless you can think of a way for us to get hitched before our time here comes to an end...' She let her words trail off and raised a shoulder in pretend disappointment.

'The captain,' he said with a gleam.

'What about him?'

'Some ship captains have the power to conduct weddings. If yours has the requisite powers, he can marry us. Does he?'

'I don't know.'

'Let's ask him.' Unthreading his fingers from her hair, Gianni ran them down her slender, golden arms. 'I assume you have your passport on board?'

'It's right here in my cabin... What a shame you don't have yours,' Issy added with fresh pretend disappointment.

'Oh, but I do,' he said triumphantly, patting his back pocket. 'I always carry it with me.'

So he wanted to drag this absurd game out did he? 'Then let me get mine.'

Issy retrieved her passport from the handbag she kept it in, lifted the receiver of the cabin's phone, which connected to all the different parts of the yacht, and smiled beatifically at Gianni. 'Shall I call the captain then?'

Thoroughly enjoying himself, Gianni nodded. 'Tell him to meet us in the lounge.'

Gianni watched her press the captain's number, certain she'd slam the receiver down before the call connected and put a halt to this charade. It was ludicrous to think they could marry. Almost as ludicrous as Issy's declaration that she was waiting for marriage. Still, she'd upped the ante of their game superbly. He'd twisted and she'd matched. He couldn't wait to watch her fold.

But she didn't fold. Instead she politely asked the captain to meet them in the lounge to discuss a personal issue. That was one thing he did like about her; that she spoke to the crew respectfully. Many yacht owners and charterers treated their crew like dirt; as if they were their personal slaves.

Call over, her lips curved. 'He'll meet us in the lounge now.'

He held his hand out to her. She laced her fingers through his and let him lead her down to the entertainment deck.

Captain James Caville entered the lounge at the same time as them. Not by word or gesture did he give away the fact he'd worked for Gianni for the last four years. Gianni was proud of his loyal crew. They'd transferred seamlessly to his new vessel and, when told that their boss—him—was being targeted by a hustler and to play along with the hustler's game, had risen to the challenge. It wouldn't even cross Issy's mind that Gianni and the good captain had spent more than a few evenings drinking their way through bottles of Scotch and playing Three Card Brag, or, on the occasions they were joined by other crew members, hunkered down at the poker table playing Texas Hold 'Em.

As a result of their friendship, Gianni thought he knew the captain pretty well and so was almost dumbstruck when, asked if he was allowed to officiate marriages, James nodded. 'The *Palazzo delle Feste* is registered in Bermuda and I have a Bermuda licence, so if you want me to marry you then I can. I'll just need to contact the ministry to go through the necessary requirements...' There was a beat of hesitation. 'Do you want me to do that?'

Gianni had to pull himself together quickly. He'd expected James to laugh at the request, had envisaged turning to Issy and teasing her about researching an island they could marry on and then winding her up into believing they would sail there. It had never crossed his mind that James would actually be allowed to marry them; he'd thought stories of ships captains marrying couples was an urban myth. He'd only chosen Bermuda to register the *Palazzo delle Feste* because that's where his last yacht had been registered.

Surely now was the time Issy would think this was getting out of hand and fold her cards. But instead of finding doubt or panic on her face, she simply gazed at him with challenge in her stare. She was waiting for Gianni to fold.

He'd never folded in his life.

Challenge accepted.

'Do it,' he said decisively.

James' only physical reaction to this was the slight

raising of an eyebrow. 'And when will you want the ceremony?'

Gianni winked at Issy. 'Right now would be great but I appreciate that's unreasonable so as soon as possible. If anything can be fast-tracked then do it—money is no object if palms need to be greased.'

James pulled his phone out of his pocket. 'I'll get onto it now.'

'A drink while we wait?' Gianni suggested to Issy.

The beatific smile returned. 'Champagne would be fitting.'

The honours done, eyes locked together, they toasted each other and each drank half their glass.

Come on, Issy, fold, he mentally urged her. *You know neither of us will go through with this charade.*

How much longer until Gianni roared with laughter and admitted this was all just a wind-up, Issy wondered. She almost felt sorry for the captain working so hard to make a fallacy happen, but it was only when he covered the speaker on his phone and asked for their passports that the first twinge of doubt hit her.

She sipped on her second glass of champagne telling herself not to be silly. It didn't matter how much money Gianni had to grease palms, marriage was not something that could be fast-tracked. Any minute now and the captain would regretfully tell them it couldn't be done before Gianni flew back to the UK, and then they would both pretend to be disappointed and Gianni would have no choice but to back off from her physically for the rest of their time together. She would just have to think harder for ways to entertain him. The yacht was a veritable party palace—even its name denoted that—so in theory it would be easy.

Theory though, as she'd come to learn since arriving in the Caribbean, was no guarantee of success when put into practice.

A member of the crew came in with a sheaf of freshly printed-off papers in her hand, which she gave to the captain. Still talking on the phone, he riffled through them, then beckoned Gianni over. Their voices were too low for her to hear but when Gianni's gaze directed itself to her, there was a calculation in it that stiffened her resolve not to be the one to throw her hands in the air and say this had gone too far.

Stifling laughter, she drank more of her champagne and watched him do something on his phone that she suspected involved transferring money. Excellent.

A stronger pang of doubt hit a short while later though when the captain started laughing to whoever he was now talking to on the phone. The laugh and the tone his voice had now adopted reminded Issy of her father's the time she'd been playing on the floor of his study while he'd been conducting a business deal. He'd taken that same lighter tone and laughed in the same manner right before he'd ended the call. He'd been so happy with the deal he'd concluded that he'd scooped Issy up and spun her in the air.

She caught Gianni's eye. He'd topped them both up with the last of the champagne then seated himself across from her, an ankle resting on a thigh, an arm strewn across the back of the sofa, the very epitome of nonchalance.

The devil raised his glass to her.

She raised hers right back.

'We're all set,' James said a minute later, rising from the table he'd set himself up on. 'We just need a couple of witnesses—I've sent a message to my officers—and we're good to go.'

The vaguely smug look that had been on Gianni's face while they'd waited, like that of a chess player waiting for their opponent to realise they were heading for a loss, flickered. He straightened. 'You can marry us now?'

The captain shrugged. 'It's cost you a lot of money, but I have the authorisation.'

Gianni somehow kept his features straight as he swore loudly to himself. This had gone too far. Issy *had* to fold now. He looked back at her. 'Ready to marry me?'

Eyes not leaving his face, she drained her champagne. 'Why not? Like you said, it'll be fun… Unless you have cold feet?'

'No cold feet from me.' He would *not* be the one to fold.

Two men in navy shorts and pale blue polo shirts with the same emblem as the crew had on their uniforms came into the lounge.

Gianni got to his feet. 'We need a ring.'

'Two rings.'

Issy got to her feet and realised she was a bit wobbly. Half a bottle of champagne on an empty stomach was probably not her best idea, but seeing as she was still sharp enough to recognise that, she wouldn't worry about it. This actually had become fun, and she giggled at the absurdity of it all, and giggled too, to think of Gianni wasting oodles of his money on a marriage that wouldn't take place. 'Any spare paper?' she asked the captain.

When he gave her a sheet, she knelt at a coffee cable and quickly ripped two strips off it. Each strip she rolled lengthways between her fingers until it resembled a long wriggly worm, then tied each one into a circle, which she held out to Gianni with a flourish. 'There,' she said, flashing a grin at him. 'Two makeshift wedding rings.'

'You're ready to do this?' he reiterated.

He wanted her to back out. He *expected* her to back out. She could see it in his eyes. And it was that expectation which filled her with serene defiance. Gianni had started this game of chess and it was up to him to put an end to it.

It was only when he clasped her hand and together they faced the captain that she realised neither of them was prepared to back down.

They'd reached stalemate.

Gianni had the strangest feeling of leaving his body and floating above and looking down on himself and Issy, hands clasped and reciting vows before the captain and growing number of crew come to see for themselves if the boss really was marrying the hustler. He watched himself sign the certificate where the captain told him to and watched Issy sign her name—her real name, Isabelle Christine Seymore—and the two witnesses sign theirs. Then he watched himself slide the

paper ring over her finger and Issy slide the one she'd
made for him over his finger, and continued watching
with the same detachment while they kissed to seal
their vows.

And then he re-inhabited his body as a flurry of
handshakes and embraces were shared, the heavy beats
of his heart rippling through him at the knowledge
that the game of bluff he'd just played with Issy had
backfired.

Issy popped two painkillers into her mouth with a
shaking hand and washed them down with cold water.
The after-effects of the champagne she'd drunk just a
short while ago were making themselves known in the
form of a headache. Or maybe the cause of it was the
sudden loss of the adrenaline that had pumped through
her in that mad hour that had ended with her married.

The amusement that had been carried with the
adrenaline had gone too, reality as cold as the water
she'd just drunk pouring over and through her.

She'd just married her nemesis. She hadn't merely
exchanged fake vows but signed legal documents.
Signed them in her real name. The only saving grace
was Gianni had failed to notice anything about her
surname.

But what on earth had possessed her? What had
possessed *him*?

Amelia was going to kill her...

Oh, hell, she hadn't thought of her sister in hours,
had completely forgotten about her lost phone and that

her sister would be waiting anxiously with her own phone in hand for an update. She *had* to find her phone.

Closing her eyes, Issy took some deep breaths to force a modicum of calm into herself. It was the middle of the night in London. Amelia wouldn't be worrying; that was Issy projecting. Amelia would only worry if Issy went the whole of the next day without communicating. If her phone stayed missing, she would borrow one off the crew, search the main number for Rossi Industries and call Amelia through it. Her priority, she realised with a flash, was to tell the captain to destroy the marriage papers. If they weren't lodged, they wouldn't be properly registered, ergo, the 'marriage' would never be legalised.

These things decided in her mind, she expelled a more settled breath and called the captain. Told by one of his officers that he was currently unavailable but would call her back soon, she said, 'Don't worry, I'll speak to him first thing in the morning.' They were in the middle of the Caribbean Sea. Nothing would be done with the papers before morning and Gianni was due soon to escort her to dinner. She needed to work out how she was going to play things.

It was a thought that set her heart thumping again.

How was she supposed to brazen this out? Marriage.

Not marriage, she told herself stubbornly. Just a joke, a game, whatever, that had gone a step too far. So long as the papers weren't lodged, there would be no real marriage. She was safe.

Her head sorted and the painkillers kicking in, she decided the best thing to do was continue the joke and play up the marriage, so selected a slinky white fitted dress with spaghetti straps that came just below the knee and had a slit cut into its skirt that ran almost to the top of her thigh. For her feet she chose a pair of white spaghetti strap sandals to match. With her hair blow-dried into the illusion of thickness and her eyes painted a smoky grey, she finished the look off with a smear of red lipstick.

As prepared as she thought she was though, she still needed a moment to collect herself before answering the knock on her cabin door.

Gianni stood there, wearing the same polo shirt and canvas shorts that had been draped over his too magnificent body at various times throughout the day and with that devilish smile her brain hated but which her body adored on his too gorgeous face. 'Ready for dinner, Signora Rossi?'

The longing that ran through her came close to making her legs collapse, and right in that moment Issy knew this had to end.

She couldn't handle Gianni or her feelings for him. She wasn't just in over her head, she was close to *losing* her head. She'd married him for heaven's sake! There was no way she could spend a whole week with him without losing her mind and probably the last of her self-respect. She had to trust that Amelia had done her part in the meeting that day and that their operation to destroy the Rossi cousins had reached the point of no return.

Because much more time spent with Gianni was going to push Issy to the point of no return.

She had to end this. She *would* end this.

A modicum of peace settled in her wildly fluctuating heart.

She would get their marriage papers destroyed and this horror story would end as soon as they docked on whichever the closest island was. She would insist they go off and explore and then she'd give Gianni the slip and escape without him, even if it meant abandoning the yacht.

All she needed to do was brazen things out and hold him off sexually for a few more hours.

'*Si, signor,*' she murmured, giving him a look of adoration that scarily needed no effort whatsoever.

He held his elbow out to her.

She didn't hesitate to slip her hand through it.

His eyes gleamed. 'I don't know about you but I'm already looking forward to dessert.'

The crew had transformed the dining room into a silver and gold extravaganza. It never ceased to amaze Gianni how ingeniously creative they could be in catering to his whims, and also the whims he hadn't even expressed. How they'd got hold of balloons, glitter and confetti and decorated the room accordingly would remain a mystery. He wouldn't ask. Sometimes the mystery was enough.

The dining table, which could comfortably seat twenty people, had been laid in an L at one end, with Gianni at the head and Issy to his right. Romantic candles had been lit, the reflection of their flames dancing off the crystal chandelier above. The huge windows lining the left of the dining room added to the romantic ambience, the setting sun on the horizon turning the sky a burnished orange that made it appear to be on fire. It perfectly matched the fire taking place inside him.

Gianni raised his glass of champagne to his bride and, for at least the dozenth time since he'd turned up at her cabin, marvelled at how ravishing she looked. He could hardly believe the beautiful creature beside him was the same woman in the screenshot he'd cloned. Alone in his cabin, he'd found himself staring intently at that picture with the strangest mixture of emotions playing through him. He strongly suspected the screenshot was Issy in her natural state and this blonde vision of perfection was a carefully curated image in which to ensnare him. What he couldn't understand was why the plainer, unpolished, plumper version on the screen made his chest tighten so much.

He'd shoved the strange emotions aside while showering for dinner, shaking off, too, the strange flux that had taken him out of himself during their 'wedding ceremony.' The papers they'd signed would never see the light of day. More than an annulment, their 'marriage' would never have happened. He was confident Issy shared the same thoughts on the matter but that, like him, she'd decided to play it out. How long did she think she could do that for?

Come the morning, they would dock at St Lovells and this charade would be over.

For tonight, he would enjoy his time with this dazzling woman and see what tricks she had planned to back out of consummating the marriage that would never be.

CHAPTER EIGHT

To Issy's surprise and relief, the dinner was actually fun. As course after course of the most exquisite food was brought out to them—the chef really had pulled out all the stops to create a feast for them—they slipped into light, impersonal conversation. Neither of them even bothered faking conversation about their future together. They both knew it wouldn't happen. It didn't need to be spelt out. The subjects they did touch on, though, gave her a greater insight into the man she'd believed she knew so well before meeting him, minor things no amount of research on Gianni could have dredged up.

'You don't read?' she asked in astonishment when they moved from music they liked onto books, and he couldn't name a single one he'd enjoyed.

'Not since I left school. The books they forced us to read were too boring and worthy for me to get any enjoyment from.'

'Didn't your parents encourage you?' She thought of how both her parents had helped and encouraged her to read, sparking a love of literature in her that she'd carried all her life.

His features tightened at this. 'My father is a homo-phobic and misogynistic bully. If he'd seen me read-ing a book for pleasure he'd have probably assumed I was gay and beat me.'

Shock at this brutal admission came close to mak-ing her choke on the raspberry she'd just popped in her mouth.

From the way he grimaced and the deep breath he took, she sensed this was an admission he hadn't in-tended to make. Swirling the wine in his glass, he tipped it down his throat. 'Sorry,' he said as he refilled both their glasses. 'I didn't mean to lower the mood.'

'That's okay… Did you mean it?'

His gaze was steady. 'I would never lie about some-thing like that. My father is a monster.' The beginnings of a smile formed. 'But I don't want to talk about him on my wedding night so why don't you tell me about the books you enjoy.'

Issy had no idea why the thought of Gianni's father being a monster hurt her chest so much or why she felt something much like a yearning that he'd shut the sub-ject down. It didn't make sense. She knew the bones of his childhood—the whole world did—so why the sudden craving to know more, to have flesh put onto those bones? She knew his mother had left his father when Gianni was a child and that she lived in Milan. She knew his father ran the same family vineyard in Umbria with his brother that the Rossi cousins had been raised in and that Gianni and his cousin were both estranged from their fathers, going so far as to change their surnames when they were eighteen. It was all part of their legend as self-made men who'd risen from nothing to the stratosphere. What more did she need to know?

It frightened her that she *wanted* to know more.

For the first time since they'd entered the dining room, she had to force a smile to her face. 'There's no point in me telling you if you haven't read any of them.'

Gianni stared at her for a beat. There had been a moment when he'd been certain she was going to press him for more information about his father. Instead, she'd chosen to respect his wish to end the subject. He never spoke about his father. He wasn't worth the wasted breath. He rarely thought about him either. He wasn't worth the headspace.

To find himself thinking about both his parents in one day and to actually mention his father, to confide a snippet of his life to Isabelle Seymore of all people, was perplexing, and he rubbed his hand over the thickening stubble of his jawline. What the hell was it about her that made the past feel so much closer than it had in over a decade?

'You've read a lot of books?'

She nodded.

'Don't tell me a party girl like you is a secret bookworm?' he teased.

She put a finger to her lips. 'Secret being the operative word.'

Unable to resist, he snatched at the finger and brought it to his own lips. 'Something tells me you're full of secrets, Signora Rossi.'

Her eyes glittered, and she stroked the finger

pressed against his lips across his cheek, whispering, 'And something tells me it won't be long before you discover all of them.'

He captured her hand again and pressed a kiss into the palm. 'I look forward to it.'

The glitter darkened. 'So do I.'

An undercurrent had built, a tension laced with more than the sexual chemistry that kept drawing them so close together. Gianni could almost taste the deception swirling between them, nearing the surface, straining for the moment when their masks—already slipping—could be ripped away and nothing but the truth would be enough to satisfy them.

'What do you say to a game of snooker?' he asked.

'Only if you promise not to thrash me.'

He leaned his face close to hers. 'I never make promises I can't keep.'

Issy chalked her cue, watching as Gianni folded his huge frame to make the break. There was nothing gentle in his stroke. He hit the white ball with an accurate determination that rolled it forcefully along the table and smashed it into the red triangle of balls.

She smiled to herself. He'd played the shot like that for her benefit. Separating the red balls from their triangular cluster made it easier to pot them, not something a serious player—and she could tell from the way he played his shot that he was a serious player—would do if they didn't think their opponent would be easy pickings.

Deciding on and playing her shot quickly, she

chided herself when the red ball she'd shot at missed the pocket.

Gianni didn't miss. He potted a red, then followed it by potting the pink, then potted another red. He missed the green by millimetres, switching the game back to Issy.

This time, she took her time, angled the cue carefully and made her shot. The white glanced the red, sending it into a pocket. She followed this with four successful shots, red, green, red, brown, but then, seeing there was no way she could pocket another red from where the white ball was placed, she hit the white softly, so it only brushed against the red, then gently rolled to slip behind the pink. She'd snookered him.

The look he gave her made her feel ten foot tall. Total confounded admiration.

'I thought you didn't play?' he accused, leaning over the table to reach the white.

'I don't remember saying that,' she refuted innocently.

His chin now lined against the cue, he raised an eyebrow at her. 'You implied it.'

Smirking, she shrugged. 'I haven't played for ten years.'

He took his shot. He managed to hit the red but didn't pot it. 'How old are you?'

'You should know that seeing as you're my husband,' she teased. 'I'm twenty-three. My dad had a snooker table. I always wanted to play but I couldn't reach the table so he bought me a child-size one for my seventh birthday and taught me. I upgraded to the full-size one when I was ten.'

'How were you able to see over the top of it?' he teased back.

'I used a stool. Being so small meant the distances looked longer to me but I think that improved my game.'

'Have you actually grown at all since then?'

'Very funny.' The red she was aiming for went straight into the pocket.

'Give me a chance,' he mock-pleaded. 'Go on, make it harder to see over the table. Take your shoes off.'

'They're sandals, you philistine.'

'A philistine?' His expression suddenly changed to serious and he lost the English accent he'd clearly worked so hard to make faultless. 'I do not think it means what you think it means.'

'Inconceivable.'

Their eyes met, identical amazed gazes at the rec-ognition that they were with a fellow *Princess Bride* buff formed, and then they both started laughing. Issy laughed so hard she completely missed her next ball.

Grinning widely, Gianni took his shot and pocketed it, but missed his next one.

'Maybe I *should* take my sandals off if it gives you more of a chance,' she taunted.

His eyes drifted down her body. 'I don't know...' His voice dropped to a murmur as his gaze drifted back up to capture her eyes. 'Those sandals are very sexy.'

And just like that, the heat of awareness Issy had been vaguely dampening by sheer willpower flamed back to life, sending her heart into a pulsing mess at the strength of longing rampaging through her. If Gianni hadn't been standing on the other side of the snooker table her legs might just have propelled themselves to him.

She picked up her glass and took a long drink of her mojito, fully aware the skin on her face blazed with the same intensity as what was happening beneath it, fully aware too that Gianni knew exactly the effect those five little words had had on her.

But he didn't say anything, simply stood there waiting for her to take her turn, his cue in hand, that sensuous, knowing, *sexy* look…damn him…playing on his face.

Damn him!

Damn him too that, in order to stretch across the table and reach the white ball, she had to hitch the skirt of her tight dress up, something she'd done numerous times during their game already but which she'd done automatically, barely even thinking about it. This time, she was painfully aware of the suggestiveness that could be interpreted with the gathering of the silk, painfully aware too of how sensitive her thighs had become as the material rode up them.

Trying her hardest to control her breathing and concentrate, Issy draped herself over the table and aimed the cue.

'The rest of you is pretty damn sexy too,' he said at the exact moment she took her shot. 'Your backside is delectable.'

She misaimed the cue. The white ball scuttled off

in the wrong direction, limping to a stop without hitting anything.

That pulled her together sharpish, and she glared at him. 'You said that on purpose to distract me.'

He raised a hefty shoulder. 'And?'

'And?'

He took his position at the table and winked at her. 'And what are you going to do about it?'

God how she hated how much she wanted him. Almost as much as she hated how greatly she was coming to enjoy their time together and how she could veer from amusement to full-blown desire from nothing but a tone in his voice or the raising of an eyebrow.

'I could sing to you,' she suggested, managing to sound reasonably normal in the process. 'People have offered money to stop me doing that before.'

He grinned. 'You can come up with something better than that.' He potted the last of the reds and fixed his stare straight back on her. 'I guarantee if you were to strip that dress off, I'd be unable to take another shot.'

She squeezed her eyes to counter the image that zinged straight into her mind of holding Gianni's gaze and peeling her dress off for his delectation. She had to force her eyes to open again and force her voice to sound blasé. 'I prefer the singing option.'

Chin on cue now lined up for the next shot, he smirked. 'I don't.' The yellow ball potted straight into the pocket.

Knowing she needed to steer them onto safer conversational territory, she asked, 'How come you're so good at this? At snooker,' she hurried to clarify before he could deliberately misinterpret her question and give a suggestive answer.

He took another shot. 'I have a snooker table in my London penthouse and my home in Tuscany. I like to play.'

'That fits in with your playboy image so well.' That's what she needed to remind herself of, she realised. When the force of Gianni's magnetism and personality was strong enough to blur the damage he'd wrought on her family; made it seem distant and faded, she needed to remember the chain of broken hearts he'd left littered around the world.

'I don't have a playboy image.'

'You do! I've looked you up.' About a gazillion times. 'You have your own hashtag. HotRossi.'

'Not started by me.'

'Started by your adoring groupies. You're a playboy who loves to party.'

'It's not a crime for a single man to party and date women.'

'I'm just saying your image doesn't fit a man who must have spent hours at a snooker table to get as good as you at it.'

'Snooker helps my brain relax. It's a good way to unwind in the evenings…' His lips curved in a lopsided smirk and he wiggled his eyebrows. 'When there's no hot woman available to help me relax, of course.'

This time she was able to maintain her composure, serenely saying, 'You're trying to needle me.'

'Am I succeeding?'

'No.'

His knowing grin showed he didn't believe her. 'It would be impossible for me to have such a successful business if I partied every night. I've reached the age where I get hangovers.'

'Oh, no. You poor thing.'

'Thank you for your sympathy.'

'You're welcome.'

'You do realise I've won?'

She looked at the snooker table. While they'd been bantering, Gianni had cleared the table so only the black ball remained. She couldn't beat his score with the value of it.

'Do I get my prize?'

'What prize? You cheated,' she accused.

'No, I didn't.' He placed his cue on the table and stalked to her. 'I was observing. Your bottom really is delectable.'

Heart thumping again, she sidestepped away from him and pulled the triangle for the red balls out of the slot. 'You distracted me. Play again without cheating.'

'You call that a distraction? *Bella*, that is *nothing* on what I could have done.'

Her pelvis practically contracted at the meaning, but she kept her focus. 'I call it cheating, and you're going to play fairly this time. I'll make the break.'

Completely blurring him from her vision, Issy ordered fresh drinks over the intercom then set the table. After chalking her cue, she folded herself to take the first shot but before she could hit the cue, she forgot to keep blurring Gianni and he appeared in her line of sight. He'd removed his polo shirt. His glorious chest was naked.

His eyes gleamed as he noticed that she'd noticed. Raising his drink to her, he said in an innocent tone, 'I was getting hot.'

'Then turn the air-conditioning up.'

'And waste power unnecessarily?' He tutted in disappointment. 'Feel free to remove your own clothes if you find it hot too.'

'Shut up.' Issy gritted her teeth to concentrate and hit the white ball with just enough force for it to reach the triangle of reds without breaking them up.

Gianni stepped to the table, hardly glanced at the balls as he took his shot and smashed them. Two reds dropped into the pockets.

Within ten minutes he'd cleared the table. Other than making the opening break, Issy didn't get a single shot. It was a masterclass in snooker, as good as anything she'd watched on TV as a child.

But she'd hardly paid attention to the shots. Throughout, Gianni kept his focus entirely on the table, not looking at her once. There had been nothing for her to fight against, no sensuous glances, no velvet-delivered innuendoes...

She'd fallen into a trance, mesmerised by the raw grace of the man and the beauty of his masculinity as he'd demolished the table.

By the time he potted the black ball for the last time and, finally, lifted his eyes to her, she couldn't have torn her gaze from him if she'd tried.

A smile slowly ghosted his face. Casually placing

his cue on the table, he drained his Scotch and, with the gait and expression of a lion approaching its prey, stalked to her.

His eyes were intent, deadly, his words husky. 'I think that has earned me my prize.'

Her heart filled her chest with thick, heavy beats.

Fight or flight. That's what prey experienced when their senses registered the big cat emerging from the flora. Those semi-seconds of intuition and experience before adrenaline kicked in was the entire difference between life and death. Fight a lethal predator bigger than you and die. Take flight a moment too late and die.

There came a point when every captured prey gave up the fight and welcomed death to release them from the pain.

Gianni had captured her that night in London. She'd arrived at the club having badly underestimated the power of his sexuality and spent every waking moment since battling her own reactions to it.

She couldn't run any more. The will to fight had deserted her.

Submitting didn't mean death. Gianni wouldn't inflict pain on her, only pleasure, and for this one night, she wanted to explore where that pleasure could take them because she knew, with a marrow-deep certainty, that she could live a hundred lives and never feel what she felt for Gianni with anyone else.

Feeling a strange combination of shyness and boldness, Issy took a step towards him. 'What prize?' she whispered.

Gianni's chest swelled before he splayed a hand

against her back to draw her flush to him. Her eyes were wide and filled with the desire he caught so often in them, but they were filled with something else too that he'd never seen before, an openness, as if she'd ripped an invisibility cloak away.

He dipped his face to hers. 'You.'

As their mouths fused together, Gianni had the strangest sensation that this was Issy kissing him. Issy, the young woman in the screenshot with the ice cream sundae, not Issy the polished seductress. Whichever Issy it was, he hungered for her with a power that was coming close to taking possession of him, and as her lips and tongue danced against his, the electricity that had flickered and crackled between them the entire day magnified and fired huge jolts through his veins and deep into his loins.

Dragging his fingers down her back, he clasped the bottom he'd spent most of the day fantasising about and gathered the silk of her dress until it was high enough for him to lift her onto the snooker table.

When she opened her eyes the strange sensation hit him again, and with it the belief that he was looking into the eyes of the real Isabelle for the first time. There was nothing calculated in it. No guile. Just her. Just Issy and her desire for him.

He cupped her cheeks and kissed her so passionately she moaned into his mouth and scraped her fingers over his back. A zipper ran the length of her dress to her bottom and he pinched it and drew it down. Not breaking the lock of their mouths, she shrugged the spaghetti straps off her shoulders so they slipped down her arms and the dress fell to her waist, allowing her naked breasts to crush against his bare skin for the first time. *Dio*, he'd never known bare skin against bare skin could feel so incredible.

Breathing heavily, Gianni broke the kiss so he could gaze into her desire-drugged eyes again and drink in the heightened colour staining her cheeks.

He placed a hand to her chest and gently pressed her back. And then he brushed his hand over a breast that fitted into the palm as if it had been specially made for him. Pressing her back even further, he dipped his head and captured a dusky pink nipple in his mouth.

Issy jolted and gasped at the unexpected shock of pleasure that coursed through her. But it didn't end there, not with Gianni kissing and biting and sucking the overly sensitised skin, moving from breast to breast, flickering his tongue down lower still to nip at her navel, his hands roaming the contours of her body, fingers sliding over silk and flesh, leaving her skin flamed in their wake.

The flames deepened when his mouth found hers again and his hand slid beneath the bunched hem of her dress and grasped the band of her knickers. Thrilling at the hunger of his kisses, greedily devouring him with the same intensity, she gripped Gianni's shoulders and raised her bottom. He yanked the knickers down her thighs. A couple of flicks of her legs and they slipped down her calves to her feet, from where she kicked them off.

His desire when he pulled back to soak up her semi-nakedness, etched in every line of his hooded, heavy stare, overrode any of Issy's shyness at being displayed like this. There was a pained reverence in the look, as if she were the first woman he'd ever seen like this.

Could he see through her skin to the wildly beating heart? Could he see the flames licking her veins and bones?

One pop of a button and tug at a zip and his shorts fell down.

Issy roamed her gaze over him in the same way he'd soaked her up. She could hardly breathe. All her life, she'd thought the female body the more pleasing of the sexes. Gianni Rossi was the only man whose body had ever drawn her eye but for years she'd told herself it was because of her intensive research on him, that the reason she kept going back to pictures of him half-naked holidaying on his yacht was for whichever companion he happened to be with so she could study them in her pursuit of copying their look.

It had always been him. The devil disguised as Apollo. The sexiest man to roam the earth.

But she'd never seen a picture of him fully naked. Just as the pictures of him had never done him justice, seeing him naked was a revelation in itself. Magnificent was too lame a word to describe him. Every part of the devil was beautiful.

'Kiss me,' she whispered. There was something about his kisses that fed her hunger and made her greedy for more. Much more. Greedy for everything.

In a flash their mouths locked back together. Hands dragged heavily over skin, a need to discover and taste pulsing through them both, pulses that turned into throbs when Gianni cupped her sex and pressed his thumb against her swollen nub. Dear heavens, she'd thought it had felt good earlier… That was nothing… nothing.

She rubbed against him, moaning her pleasure into the deepening tangle of tongues.

Gianni could hardly believe how hot and wet Issy was for him. If the cells of the human body could make sound, hers would be crying out their need. He could feel it, taste it, smell it, and, keeping the pressure on the source of her pleasure, slipped a finger inside the sticky heat, his senses thrumming as her moans deepened and she clung even tighter to him.

Panting, she broke the fusion of their mouths and, still rocking into him, almost bit his cheek as she gasped, 'Condoms?'

He could hardly speak. 'In my pocket.'

'Get…' But her words died. Her eyes glazed, her pants shortened and suddenly her neck arched and her mouth opened. No sound came out. It didn't need to. Issy's silent climax shuddered through her, its ripples practically visible, and suddenly the need to take possession and lose himself inside her peaked to the point of desperation.

Only when he was certain that she'd passed her own peak did he gently remove his hand and kiss her. 'Let me get the condom.'

'Do it,' she whispered.

In a flash, he pulled a condom out of his back pocket, ripped the packet with his teeth and sheathed himself. Her hands were reaching for him, and when he stepped between her legs, she clasped the back of his neck.

He guided his erection to her damp opening.

Still breathing heavily, she swallowed and huskily said, 'Be gentle, okay?'

He jerked a nod, gripped a hip and, with anticipation almost too heavy to bear, was about to press himself inside her sticky heat when it flashed in his mind: the question *why* she would ask him to be gentle. 'Is this your first time?' He had to drag the words out.

Her grip tightened on his neck and she pushed back, encouraging him to take possession. His arousal throbbed so hard it burned through every part of him. 'Yes,' she breathed.

How desperately he wanted to thrust himself inside her. It was a desperation he'd never felt before. Not like this.

She was a virgin.

'It's okay,' she said raggedly, bringing her mouth to his and scraping the pads of her fingers over the bristles on the back of his neck. 'You won't hurt me.'

Her simple declaration landed like a punch to his solar plexus.

His confession came from nowhere. 'I know who you are.'

CHAPTER NINE

Issy was so consumed with the incredible feelings building on the tendrils of her climax and heightened anticipation for Gianni to take that final step and take possession of her that his words simply bounced like music through her head.

She wanted to experience everything, feel everything, lose herself in the hedonism of Gianni's touch…

But he was no longer moving. The fusion that would take her to heaven had stopped before it had properly started.

'Is something wrong?' she whispered, brushing her lips over his, trying to discern why his eyes were squeezed so tightly shut and his jaw clenched.

He breathed heavily through his nose before his eyes opened. His throat moved before he hoarsely repeated, 'I know who you are.'

Understanding seeped slowly into her dazed brain, and she had to blink a number of times to help clear it. 'You know…?'

'I know you're Thomas Seymore's daughter.'

But still her brain refused to fully comprehend. His

words made no sense… Not until ice began to creep its way up her spine and through her chest, and the breaths she'd struggled to find in the throes of passion became lodged in her throat and lungs.

The dazedness in her head melted and swam, white lights flickering, the ice in her body spreading until comprehension hit her fully and the breath exploded out of her. Slamming her fists against his chest, Issy pulled her thighs up and together, then twisted to one side and dropped off the table. Her feet slammed onto the floor, but she'd forgotten she was still wearing the stupidly high sandals and her ankle buckled at the impact, making her fall.

In an instant he was at her side, concern written all over his face.

Frantically trying to cover her modesty with the dress that until moments ago had been bunched around her waist, she huddled into herself. 'Get away from me.'

'Issy…'

She wanted to spit in his face. 'I said get away from me. Get out. Get out now.'

'Issy, please…'

'Get out!' she screamed, losing all control of herself. 'Get out, get out, get *out*!'

His broad shoulders rose and his chin lifted. Tension lined his face and made his body appear carved from stone.

She couldn't bear to look at him a moment longer and buried her face in her knees. She thought she might be sick.

As much as she tried to tune him out, she was acutely aware of movement around her and stiffened when a breeze feathered over her bowed head and the slightest pressure brushed against her hair.

She sensed rather than heard Gianni leave the games room. The emptiness he left in his wake confirmed he'd gone.

Gianni splashed cold water on his face and tried to regulate his breathing. Guilt pulsed strongly inside him.

Gripping tightly to the sink, he dragged air into his lungs and tried to banish the image of Issy, humiliated and vulnerable, huddled on the floor.

The game they'd been playing had come to its conclusion but he'd been incapable of playing the final round.

He knew he'd done nothing wrong. *He* was the innocent party in all this. Issy had been playing him long before their first encounter, a meeting *she'd* engineered. Everything that had followed had been by her design. Everything. She'd played herself off as a socialite party girl and seduced him with her eyes and words. She'd even blagged his own yacht as a prop for her game. All he'd done was play along. Even when he'd learned her true identity and discovered she'd set all this up as part of a plan to destroy him and his cousin, the worst he'd done was hide her phone.

Yes. He was the innocent party in all this so why he should have had that awful paralysis of guilt when they were finally acting on the desire that had sparked at their very first meeting was inexplicable. And why he should still feel that guilt lying so heavily inside him was doubly so.

Issy peeked out of her cabin's curtains. The sun was rising, the last remaining stars twinkling before daylight extinguished them. The *Palazzo delle Feste* was already cutting its way through the Caribbean Sea.

She took a deep breath and put an internal call—the only calls her cabin phone could make—through to the captain.

By the time the call ended, despair had her in its grip.

The marriage papers were already lodged with the ministry.

Gianni showered and dressed. He'd spent the night in his own cabin. He'd been looking forward to spending his first night in it—sleeping in an opulent room with all the amenities a man could need, knowing how hard he'd worked for it and that no one could take it from him was a thrill that never grew old—but he'd been unable to settle. Sleep had been elusive. Every time he closed his eyes, it was Issy he saw, huddled on the floor, humiliated and vulnerable.

He'd put the order through to set sail for St Lovells before the sun had even risen and asked for the marriage papers to be destroyed. The captain had been able to comply with the first request. It was the second that was a problem. Believing the happy couple wanted the papers lodged as soon as possible, the captain had paid—well, Gianni had paid—for a member of the ministry to take a speedboat to the *Palazzo delle Feste* and collect the documents. Working back through the time line, Gianni estimated the official had arrived when he and Issy had been in the games room. All the crew had been under his strict instructions not to enter or disturb them unless specifically asked. Worse still, the bribed official had already lodged the papers. To disentangle them from their joke of marriage would now take an annulment.

That would teach him to give someone else power to spend his own money without limits, he thought wearily.

The marriage disentanglement was something that could wait. For now, it was Issy at the forefront of his mind. He knew he shouldn't care about her state of mind but that didn't stop his chest sharpening every time her image flashed in his head. Seeing as that was every other second, his chest felt like it had an ice pick jammed in it.

He found her on the sundeck, dressed in a long-sleeved sheer white kaftan eating her breakfast. She looked different, her hair tied in a loose ponytail, not a scrap of make-up on her face. She looked younger.

Breathing deeply to quell the tempest raging in his stomach, Gianni put his phone on the table and took the seat across from her. She didn't look at him, concentrating on the plate of eggs on toast with sides of bacon and mushrooms she was steadily making her way through, pausing only to pour herself more coffee from the cafetière. She added cream from the jug then a heaped spoonful of sugar, stirred vigorously, took a sip and then picked her cutlery back up and continued to eat.

Helping himself to coffee and a selection of the fruit, yogurt and pastries also laid out on the table but untouched by Issy, he had to force the food down his throat and into his stomach. He had no appetite.

'How long are you going to ignore me for?' he asked when her plate was empty and he could no longer tolerate the silence.

She responded by helping herself to a chocolate croissant and pretending not to hear him.

'I appreciate you are angry with me but you only have yourself to blame. You hustled me, Issy. You brought me here to distract me so your sister could set a bomb off in my company.'

That made her still. For a moment he thought she would speak but the moment passed when she took another bite of her croissant.

'I know this will disappoint you but your plans have been thwarted. I warned my cousin as soon as I discovered what the two of you were up to.'

There was the slightest flicker on the face that still refused to look at him.

'I knew in London that you were a hustler,' he continued conversationally. 'So I cloned your phone. Once I realised what you and your sister were up to, I had your phone locked away in my cabin. I will return it to you when this is all over and there is no longer danger in allowing you to communicate with Amelia.'

She pushed her chair back from the table and got

to her feet. Still not even acknowledging his presence, she plucked an apple from the fruit platter and stepped away.

A flash of anger scalded him. 'I suppose I shouldn't be surprised at your silence. Your father had little to say for himself either when Alessandro and I confronted him with his corruption.'

For the beat of a moment her foot hovered in mid-air before she spun around and, ponytail swishing, stormed back to the table and grabbed hold of Gianni's phone. Moving too quickly for him to react, she raced to the railing and hurled it overboard.

Open-mouthed, hardly able to credit what she'd just done, Gianni watched Issy stroll back inside without once turning back to look at him.

Fury like she'd never known raged through Issy as she stormed over to the first member of the crew she came across. Realising her anger must make her look like a harpy, she took a deep breath before saying, 'Excuse me, but can I borrow your phone please? I still can't find mine.'

Leanne, probably even younger than Issy, bit her lip and dropped her stare.

Confused at her reaction, Issy put a hand to Leanne's arm. 'Are you okay? I'll pay for any roaming fees.'

Leanne shook her head. 'I can't. It's more than my job's worth.'

'What, lending me your phone? What do you mean?'

'We've all been ordered not to lend you our phones if you ask,' she mumbled.

'Ordered by who?' But she knew. Who else could it be?

'Mr Rossi.'

Issy gritted her teeth and filled her lungs to stop herself biting poor Leanne's head off. 'Look, Leanne, it doesn't matter what orders Gianni has given you. This is *my* charter. Please, let me use your phone, just for five minutes. Please.'

But the young woman only shook her head. 'This is your charter, but he's my boss.'

That swimming feeling in her head she'd experienced in the games room when she'd finally comprehended that Gianni knew exactly who she was started up again. She was almost afraid to say, 'Your boss? How?'

Eyes laden with sympathy met hers. 'Because this is his yacht.'

Issy's cabin phone rang. She glared at it. She'd spent the last hour locked away in here glaring at it, hating it for its refusal to dial out of the yacht. It was taking everything she had to maintain her fury because she knew the minute it started leaching out of her, terror for her sister was going to grab her.

Scrambling across the bed she'd been glaring at the phone from, she lifted the receiver and snapped, 'Yes?'

'Miss Seymore?'

Recognising the captain's voice, she closed her eyes and strove for a gentler tone. Much as she wanted to scream and shout at him, the captain had only been obeying orders from his real boss. 'Yes, Captain Caville. What can I do for you?'

'I thought you should know we'll be docking in twenty minutes.'

'Where?'

'St Lovells.'

'Is that an island?'

'Yes.'

'I've never heard of it…but thank you for letting me know.'

'You're welcome.' He hesitated before adding, 'My apologies again for the confusion about the wedding papers.'

But no apology for leading her on and letting her believe she'd chartered the *Palazzo delle Feste* for real when all the time he was working under Gianni's orders.

The entire crew worked for Gianni. The yacht belonged to Gianni. He'd played her like a puppet-master with sole control of the strings.

Oh, why hadn't she listened to her gut when David had shown her the *Palazzo delle Feste*? On some basic level that went beyond fear of not being able to pull off Silicon Valley or oligarch rich, she'd known the yacht was too much for what she needed. She'd known the charter was worth far too much for David to hand it over for free.

Desperation had made her ignore her gut. The window for her and Amelia to enact their revenge would only stay open for a strictly limited time and, once closed, the opportunity would likely never come again.

She'd ruined everything.

Putting the receiver back in its cradle, Issy covered her face. She mustn't cry. Not yet. Just as she wouldn't allow herself to think of how deeply wounded…broken… Gianni had left her last night. The tears would have to wait. The only thing she could allow herself to focus on was escaping Gianni. Once she'd accomplished that, she'd find a way to contact Amelia, not to warn her—she knew in her heart it was too late for that—but to make sure she was okay. That she was safe.

Both Rossi cousins were ruthless but it was Alessandro Issy found the most frightening. Unlike his cousin who the press adored, Alessandro stayed firmly out of the spotlight and so there were very few pictures of him online. Those there were showed a handsome but darkly menacing-looking man, the kind you crossed at your peril. His face perfectly matched the image Issy had conjured for him all those years ago when he and Gianni had walked out of their family home with all the swagger of a couple of gangsters who'd put a bullet in their mortal enemy. As far as Issy was concerned, they might as well have done. At least it would have spared her father a year of torment.

When she'd first seen a picture of Gianni, it had taken her a while to compute that the handsome man smiling so gregariously at the camera could be the same man who'd done and said such cruel things to her father. She'd had no such issue with Alessandro.

For all that, she'd thought Amelia was safe working for the Rossi cousins. Rossi Industries employed a hundred thousand people. Of course, only a fraction of them worked at The Ruby, the moniker given due to the pink tinge of the magnificent skyscraper the Rossi cousins had created in the heart of London as their head office, but there was safety in numbers.

Issy's negligence had put her sister in danger. She must have been negligent and overlooked something, or how could Gianni have got the measure of her so quickly?

Peering out of her cabin window, her spirits lifted the tiniest of fractions to see the small island they were sailing to. Very small. Too small for an airport but if it was big enough to dock a yacht of this size then that had to be a good thing. Her spirits lifted a fraction more to catch glimpses of pretty dwellings amongst the thick palms and verdant topography. Human life. Hopefully there would be an airfield with small charter planes. If not, there would be boats. She had emergency cash for this exact purpose. She'd known from the start that when her job was done, she'd need to make a quick escape.

It killed her to know the job would never be done. She'd blown it.

She waited until the yacht docked before slipping her feet into her rose-pink flips-flops—she would never wear heels again—and unlocked her cabin door. Satisfied the corridor was empty, she wheeled her suitcase down it. If she could make it to the metal stairs that would be unfolded for them onto the jetty without bumping into Gianni, there was a good chance she'd be able to reach safety without any further interaction with him.

The sun was high when she stepped out onto the deck, a warm breeze immediately blowing her hair around her face. She wished she'd kept her hair tied back in the ponytail, wished too that hadn't chucked her shades in her suitcase. She didn't want to waste time searching for them, not when escape was so close.

Members of the crew stood at the top of the stairs. Part of her wanted to snarl at them like a wounded cat, but she knew that impulse was unfair. Not only was Gianni their boss but his magnetism was such that even she'd come close to falling under his spell, so she fixed a smile to her face and thanked them for taking such good care of her.

About to take the first step on the stairs, a shift in the atmosphere made her hesitate. Despite the promise she'd made to herself to just leave and not look back, she turned her head before she could stop herself.

Gianni had appeared.

The punch to her heart was even stronger than the punch that had come close to flooring her when he'd joined her for breakfast.

In three long strides he was at her side and enveloping her in a fresh cloud of his gorgeous cologne. 'Let me take that for you,' he said. Before she had time to react he'd lifted the suitcase from her hand and set off down the steps and onto the jetty.

Knowing that to open her mouth and speak would

unleash the hellfire burning inside her, Issy had no choice but to follow him.

He walked purposefully, not looking back. The length and speed of his stride meant she had no chance of keeping up, so she set off at her own pace after him. If he refused to give the suitcase back then so be it. She had a bum-bag around her waist with her passport, bank cards and all her cash in it.

As she walked the long jetty, she tried to take in her surroundings. The harbour was small, only a handful of gleaming yachts moored. There were a few impossibly glamorous people in teeny bikinis and swim shorts milling around, all admiring the superyacht and no doubt trying to work out who the disembarking passengers were.

Issy tried so hard to take everything in but her eyes kept betraying her, seeking Gianni instead of seeking possible routes off this beautiful and clearly exclusive island.

He'd changed out of the familiar polo shirt and canvas shorts into a short-sleeved black shirt untucked over smart tan shorts that landed mid-thigh and a pair of brown deck shoes. He might have worn them at breakfast but she couldn't remember. She'd been too intent on comfort eating and keeping herself together to even dare look at him. Then, as now, she couldn't decipher the mountain of emotions thrashing through her. Too many. Too frightening to contemplate.

Seeing the fresh clothes he wore only heaped more humiliation on her. Gianni had embarked the *Palazzo delle Feste* with nothing but the clothes on his back and the items contained in his shorts' deep pockets. He must have had a stash of clothes locked away in the master cabin she'd been forbidden, by the owner, from entering. Forbidden by Gianni.

How she wished her heart didn't make such ripples to see the muscles of his calves tighten as he walked and the bunching of the muscles across his back.

And, when Gianni reached the end of the jetty and turned his gaze on her as he waited for her to join him, how she wished the burning ache he'd ignited inside her would douse itself to ash.

For the first time since she'd huddled on the floor of the games room, she was helpless to stop herself from meeting his eye. What she found in his glittering stare only compounded the ripples in her heart, a mirror of the tortured emotions racking her. For one mad moment, a longing ripped through her, for Gianni to cup her face in his hands and press his firm lips to hers and...

It all happened so quickly that there was no time for her to react. A man she hadn't noticed hovering beside Gianni grabbed hold of her suitcase at the exact same moment Gianni swept her into his arms and deposited her in the back of a black four-by-four car she'd also failed to notice. He quickly folded himself in beside her. The door closed.

'What are you doing?' Issy squealed, scurrying to the other door and immediately tugging on the handle. Panic gripped her harder when she found it locked. 'Let me out!'

'Soon.' He tapped on the dark window dividing them from the front of the car.

'Let me out, *now*!' The car started moving. Throwing herself forwards, Issy banged on the dividing window. 'Stop the car!'

'They won't stop.'

She banged again, harder. The glass must be reinforced otherwise her fist would probably have smashed through it.

'We're going to my complex. We'll be there in a few minutes.'

She glared at him and snarled, 'I'm not going anywhere with you.'

He sighed as if already weary of her anger and rubbed his hand over his ever-thickening stubble. 'The travel of this car says differently.'

'If you don't stop this car and let me out this minute I'll report you for kidnap.'

'Any report will have to wait until you leave St Lovells. I'm afraid you will stay here with me until I have word from my cousin that any damage you and your sister have caused our business has been contained and mitigated.'

'You can't do that!'

'I can and I will. It's not for ever, and I give you my word no harm will come to you.'

'As if I'd believe a single word that came out of your mouth,' she spat.

'That, I believe, is a classic example of a pot calling a kettle black.'

The look Issy gave him reminded Gianni of a wildcat that once made the mistake of hanging around his childhood farmhouse. This was before his mother left so he'd been nine at the most, but he remembered trying to befriend it and having a set of claws swipe his face in response. His bleeding face hadn't stopped him screaming and begging his father not to drown it. His father had proceeded to drop the cat in the well and then smack Gianni so hard around the back of his head that he'd actually seen the stars beloved of cartoon characters.

'You *can't* keep me here against my will. There are laws, you know.'

He almost felt sorry for her. '*Bella*, I *can* keep you here. I can keep you here because this island belongs to me and there is no way for you to leave without my permission.'

CHAPTER TEN

GIANNI HAD EXPOSED Issy for the conniving charlatan hell-bent on his destruction that she was, so why the emotions that passed like a reel over her face made his stomach clench made no sense. The tenderness that kept slamming into him, the longing to gather her tightly and swear on all that was holy that he would never let harm come to her…it could only be caused by sleep deprivation. He should never have spent those insomniac hours looking through the data he'd cloned from her phone. So few contacts. So few photos. So few signs that this young woman had any form of a life that could be called sociable.

He'd read the messages between her and her sister hoping to learn more about their plans but there had been little more to be gleaned, and in any case it was the photos he kept coming back to. Every woman Gianni had dated catalogued every aspect of her life with selfies. He'd got so used to it that he barely even noticed their phones being permanently turned towards themselves. Issy had thirty-three photos stored on her phone. The ice cream sundae screenshot was the oldest. A handful of others were of her sister, who looked no different to the woman he'd last seen at The Ruby barely a week ago.

The first signs of Issy's weight loss began around the time Amelia started work at Rossi Industries, book-marked in a series of photos of her smiling brightly with various equally smiley children. Her hair was that beautiful deep chestnut in every picture so he guessed she must have dyed it for their first meeting. So intent had he been on studying Issy and gauging from the timestamps that it had taken her four months to reach the size she still maintained that it was a while before he noticed all the photos were taken in a hospital and that many of the children captured had little or no hair.

'You own this island?' she whispered in horror, backing herself against the door on her side.

'Don't worry, your research skills didn't let you down.' Why he should want to reassure her on this aspect was anyone's guess. 'I brought St Lovells two years ago. I got all involved in the sale to sign a non-disclosure agreement to keep my name secret from the press—I know I can't keep it secret for ever, but I hope to enjoy it for a short while in peace. Your research skills didn't let you down with the *Palazzo delle Feste* either. The company I employed to build it also signed an NDA for the same reasons. It doesn't matter if they discover it's mine now—I've had anti-paparazzi tech-nology embedded into it.'

'Since when has being in the press bothered you?'

He shrugged. 'The press are like the hangovers I've been getting since I turned thirty—wearisome.'

'Maybe you shouldn't court them then,' she suggested tartly.

'I don't court them, I engage with them, and always for business reasons. Believe me, I have never invited the paparazzi to send a drone over my yacht to take photos of me.'

'No, that would be your girlfriends.'

'My lovers,' he corrected. 'Girlfriend implies a form of permanence.'

Something spasmed across her face at his mention of the word lover. 'Don't worry, no woman would ever be stupid enough to date you thinking it could lead to for ever.'

But Issy knew more than a few of his lovers—hateful, hateful word—would have entered a relationship with him with their eyes wide open only to be dazzled and then blinded by the light he exuded. She'd had years to prepare and protect herself against his sexual magnetism but the reality of Gianni in the flesh had penetrated the thick stone wall she'd built.

'I should hope not,' he murmured, then looked outside the window. 'This island is the perfect sanctuary. There's tourist development on one side but it's limited. I've taken the south side for my personal use. There is no docking without permission. Any journalist stupid enough to send a drone over the island can expect to have it shot down.'

'And any kidnap victim can expect to receive zero help.'

'You will have half the island to explore and do as you wish in.'

'Great, does that mean I can swim to the nearest island?'

He pulled a face. 'If you like but I wouldn't rate your chances. Even the strongest long-distance swimmer would find it a challenge swimming forty kilometres without support.'

'You can't do this, Gianni. You know you can't.'

'How many times do I have to tell you that I can? And, please, stop with the outrage. What the hell did you think would happen if I found out what you were up to? You're a clever woman—you must have imagined the scenario.'

Feeling her temper rising, Issy closed her eyes and took a deep breath. 'Where's my sister?'

'In Italy with Alessandro.'

'Voluntarily?'

'I have no idea.'

'It can't be voluntary. She'd never go anywhere alone with that beast.'

His gaze swiftly darkened. 'Do not speak of my cousin in that way.'

'Or what? You'll hit me?'

He blinked as if surprised she would even suggest such a thing. 'Never.'

'Then what? Your cousin is a monster and you are too, and I want proof my sister is safe.'

'I would give you proof if you hadn't thrown my phone into the sea.'

'Give me my phone back then so I can call her.'

'No.'

'*Please*, Gianni. Please. Keep me locked in a dark

basement with spiders if you must but please, let me call my sister. *Please*.'

It was the distress on her face that made Gianni come within a whisker of granting her request. When a solitary teardrop rolled down her cheek he had to clench his fist to stop from reaching into his back pocket for her phone.

'*Bella*, listen to me,' he said gently. 'Your sister is safe, I swear it. Alessandro is not the monster you believe him to be. He would never harm a hair on her head.'

Chin wobbling, her teeth grazed her bottom lip. 'You expect me to believe you?'

He brushed a finger across her cheek and gave a rueful smile. 'I expect nothing, but on this I want you to put your trust in me and believe me when I say Amelia is safe and no harm will come to her.'

He could not fathom why, after staring intently into his eyes for so long it felt as if she'd delved into a lifetime of his memories, her soft nod and the loosening of her taut frame as she whispered, 'Okay,' should make his chest fill so strongly.

She must be mad. Issy knew that, gazing out of the window but with her thoughts too full to see. Trusting *him*? Trusting the devil? And it wasn't because she had no choice in the matter, it was a trust that came from her heart, a relief that spread through her and eased the tightness in her lungs. It was a trust she felt guilty for having, almost as guilty as she felt when she remembered how close she'd come to giving her virginity to the devil. If Gianni hadn't confessed to knowing who she was, she would have let him make love to her, and gladly. That he'd obviously had a fit of guilt himself to make such a confession at such a time should not mean anything. He'd led her on to that point. Every word he'd said had been a lie.

But every word you've said has been a lie too…

That's different, she argued with herself. Gianni was a corrupt…she almost called him a monster but for some stupid reason her brain recoiled from allowing her to think it. But he was definitely corrupt! He was the corrupt bastard who'd stolen her father's business and destroyed her life. He deserved everything she and Amelia had been planning for him.

Are you sure about that…?

Shut up! she shouted to her stupid brain. Of course she was sure! Amelia had discovered proof of their corruption and her sister wouldn't lie.

But why did you refuse to go ahead with the plan without proof?

Because I needed to be certain we were doing the right thing! They both had been! They had agreed from the off that they wouldn't go ahead without proof that it wasn't only their father the Rossi cousins had destroyed!

Why was she having this argument with herself again? Before meeting Gianni, as Amelia's side of the plan had been gaining speed, Issy had put her fresh insistence that Amelia find proof of corruption down to cold feet. Secret doubts had gathered, and she'd become increasingly needful of something concrete and physical to throw at the Rossi cousins if it ever came to it, a certainty that this wasn't just the vengeance of two adolescent girls who'd probably been blind to their father's faults.

It was working at the hospital, she was sure, that had put those doubts about her father in her head, and she hated herself for them, would never admit to Amelia that they even existed.

Working on the children's ward meant Issy spent a lot of time with parents whose precious children hovered between life and death. Those parents were fallible. Human. But the children never saw them like that. Their children trusted them implicitly. If Mummy or Daddy said they were going to get better then they unfailingly believed them, even if that assurance was a lie. Not one parent lied out of callousness but because they couldn't bear to deal with the consequences of the truth, both to their child and to themselves.

'We're here.'

Issy blinked herself out of her reverie and looked at her watch. Only ten minutes had passed since Gianni had kidnapped her into the back of his car and she hadn't paid any attention to her surroundings.

They'd stopped at an electric gate with a guarded security box built into a high stone wall that ran as far as the eye could see either side. The narrow road they'd taken continued on the other side of the of gate, surrounded by thick, tropical foliage. As they travelled it she tried not to marvel at the beauty surrounding them but when they emerged through it and the stunning vista revealed itself, she was unable to stop the gasp that escaped her lips.

A huge cove with the clearest turquoise water she'd ever seen lapped onto the cleanest, whitest sand she'd ever seen. The rays from the sun high above them made the water and sand sparkle like a billion tiny jewels had been scattered over it. Virtually hidden amongst the palm trees lining the beach was a handful of thatched roofed chalets. The central one, set back from the other four and easily the size of them all combined, rose like a Tibetan monastery.

It was the most stunning sight she'd seen in her life, beautiful enough to make her heart twist and then pump with a sigh.

The driver parked in a sheltered garage hidden from the naked eye.

'Let me show you around,' Gianni said quietly.

Issy closed her eyes before following him out of the car.

Close-up, the complex was even more stunning than it had been from a distance.

'This is the first time I've come here since the work was completed,' he told her as they neared the chalets, each larger and set further apart from the others than she'd originally thought. Reaching the first, she realised each chalet was set in its own private landscape.

'My original intention for this holiday was to spend a week sailing on the *Palazzo delle Feste* and the second week here,' he added when she made no response.

'You've spent an enormous amount of money on something you'll only use for two weeks of the year,' she observed as he guided her past a swimming pool that looked as if it were naturally created. Palms offered natural shade on one side of it, the other a sunbather's paradise.

'I'm planning for the future.'

'Oh?'

They'd reached the grounds of the second chalet. Leading her up the path to reach it, he explained, 'I work an average of eighty-hour weeks. I've worked those kind of hours since I was a kid. At some point in the future I will want to take my foot off the brake.'

'My heart's bleeding. Still, it's your money. You can spend it how you want.'

'You're too kind.'

'I know… Although I do wonder how you can be so free with it knowing everything you have came from stealing from my father.'

'We didn't steal from your father,' he bit back.

'Yes, you did.' She wanted to glare at him but her face wouldn't cooperate, the swell of emotions rising through her made her chin wobble and her voice tremble. 'I was there, Gianni. You invited yourself into our home and took everything we had from us. You ripped the business my father had spent his life building away from him and belittled and humiliated him. You didn't just steal his business—*you destroyed everything*.'

The darkness of his stare almost made her quail. When he finally spoke, there was an ice in his tone she'd never heard before. 'Your father stole from *us*. He sold us land unfit for development and bribed surveyors and officials to cover it up. It was our first business deal and we'd worked our backsides off from the age of twelve to pay for it *and* took a loan to make up the shortfall. Thanks to your father, we were left with crippling repayment charges for land that was worthless. It took us years of working every hour God sent to make those repayments and build a nest with which to start again, and the day we took control of your father's business and kicked him into the long grass remains the best day of my life. He deserved everything, had had it coming for years, not just for how he treated us but all the other businesses and individuals he'd ripped off over the years.' He threw the chalet door open. 'This is for your personal use. Do as you please.'

And with that, he strode back down the path, tension practically vibrating from his taut gait.

Gianni was too angry to appreciate anything about the sprawling lodge he one day intended to spend half of each year living in. He toured it fighting to stop himself from snarling at the housekeeper, who must have spent hours making everything shine so brightly and kept giving him anxious looks as if afraid he was about to explode.

It took a lot to make him lose his temper. His father was a squat bundle of aggression who used his fists as weapons and his tongue as a whip. Gianni had lived with him for eighteen years, but that aggression had neither been inherited nor rubbed off on him. If it had, he would have fought it with every fibre of his being. That didn't mean he disliked or avoided confrontation, just that the anger that could make a person's face go red and voice rise and words—often regretted after—splutter from his mouth rarely worked its way through him.

Issy's accusation that he'd stolen her father's business had slashed open a wound that had been sealed a decade ago when he and Alessandro had ousted him. It had taken every ounce of control to stop his voice from rising and to stop himself leaning right into Issy's face to shout his home truths and rip the blinkers from her eyes.

There had been no stealing. If Thomas Seymore had run his business legitimately they would never have been able to take it from him. They would never have needed to.

It had been the contempt in her stare while she'd thrown the accusation at him that had bit more than her words. Contempt laced with pain. Biting more than that had been the absolute certainty that she believed it. That Isabelle Seymore believed him a thief, that she believed him *capable* of being a thief. And corrupt. Mustn't forget that. He hoped like hell Alessandro had got to the bottom of the slanderous proof of corruption Amelia had messaged Issy about.

Alone in his master suite, he sat on the bed and rubbed his temples.

It shouldn't matter what Issy thought of him. It shouldn't matter that she hated him. He had no business feeling sick to the pit of his stomach that taking the business from Thomas Seymore had affected his youngest daughter so greatly. That was on Seymore. He was the father. It had been his duty to protect his children.

Gianni grunted a morose laugh and fell back. Spreading his arms out over the mattress, he gazed up at the ceiling. Fathers were supposed to protect their children. Mothers were too. The only person Gianni and his mother had needed protecting from was his father, and then his mother had run away and left him to take the blows and bullying alone.

Issy was refusing to leave her cabin. She'd asked the staff to provide her with food she could cook for herself and then locked the door. All this had been reported to Gianni, who was glad of it. In the short space of time that he'd known Isabelle Seymore she'd managed to get under his skin and dredge up memories of a past he preferred not to remember in any detail.

The tourist part of St Lovells was an exclusive resort he'd had built when he bought the island. Already it had gained a reputation as the ultimate luxury retreat for wealthy young things looking for a good time. Gianni was on his one full holiday of the year, the break he took annually to recharge his batteries and he was damned if he was going to let Issy's sulking prevent him from enjoying himself, not when it was her connivance that had stopped him making the usual plans in the Caribbean. On a normal holiday, he would hook up with a group of friends who spent their summers bumming around the Caribbean, invite along his latest lover to join them and generally have a great time doing nothing but enjoy himself for fourteen days.

He'd had a good night's sleep and now he was ready to enjoy himself and party. Issy could stay in her cabin and sulk for the duration of their stay here if she so wished but he was not going to let it stop him having fun.

The number of visitors was kept strictly limited, not as a means of keeping people out but as a means of preserving the island's natural beauty. One thing he'd learned in his career as a property developer was that there was always a trade-off when making a development between what humans needed and what the planet's other inhabitants needed. He much preferred developing on sites that had already been in use or on land that was ecologically worthless. The land they'd bought off Thomas Seymore was in the latter category, although just how worthless had been kept hidden from them until it was too late to do anything about it. The land Gianni's father and uncle owned containing the vineyards Gianni and his cousin had been forced to toil on throughout their childhood was heading the same way. Their fathers were ravaging the land, literally running their business into the ground.

When Gianni bought St Lovells he'd had a clear idea of how it would be developed: minimally. The work on both the tourist part and his private complex had been completed with ninety-five percent of the island left untouched. It was a tropical paradise alive with noisy, colourful wildlife, and as he took a golf buggy—his four-by-four was the only full-size motor vehicle allowed on the island—to the tourist part on his second day there, the darkness of his mood lifted.

One day, he would force his cousin to visit. Alessandro never took time off. The man was a machine. It still amazed him how two boys who were born only months apart, shared so much of the same DNA and had been raised like brothers could be so different and yet remain so close. Gianni would take a bullet for his cousin and he knew Alessandro would do the same for him.

He suspected Issy's relationship with her sister was similar. He didn't know Amelia well but knew she was a different kind of personality to her sister, more focused and analytical, more introverted. Issy had tried to hide her real self beneath the fake, polished exterior she'd projected to entrap him and portray herself as someone completely different to who she was, but he'd caught enough glimpses of the real Issy and studied enough of her photos and messages to know she was a smiley, kind, good person.

He stopped the buggy and rested his head back. Closing his eyes, he took a long breath. Issy had dedicated many years of her life to working against him, building a plan to ensnare him into a distraction so her sister could bring down his company. Good, kind people did not behave in that way. Just because she was a nurse who worked with sick children did not make her an angel.

Snapping his eyes back open, he continued his drive to the tourist resort.

The main resort pool was edged with beautiful people sunbathing and drinking cocktails. He rubbed his growing beard, fixed a grin to his face, and set off to join them.

* * *

The beach party went on until the early hours. Having had too much to drink to safely drive, Gianni got one of the resort staff to drive him back to his complex. Needing air to clear his head, he walked from the security gate and reflected on what a great day it had been. As he'd expected, he was already acquainted with a number of the vacationers: a supermodel whose best friend he'd once had a fling with and her latest beau, a genius app creator who frequented many of the same clubs and bars as him in London. They'd greeted him like an old friend and quickly introduced him to the rest of the party they were vacationing with, bright shiny, rich and beautiful twenty-somethings. One of them had been an American television actress he'd vaguely recognised, a tall, slender blonde with come-to-bed eyes she'd kept firmly fixed on him. She was exactly Gianni's type and he'd flirted with her for hours before realising his heart wasn't in it and that she didn't do anything for him. When she'd whispered in his ear on the beach about slipping away to her chalet, he'd graciously turned her down and called it a night.

He was still mulling over what it was about the actress he'd failed to respond to considering she ticked every box he wanted in a lover when he reached Issy's cabin. One of the lights was on. His heart turned over then rose up his throat, and he had to tread his feet firmly to stop them taking the path to her door.

CHAPTER ELEVEN

THE KITCHEN IN Issy's chalet was, in comparison with the rest of the place, tiny. Compared to the kitchen she shared with Amelia, it was humungous. Obviously installed with no expectation the occupier would ever use it—the staff had been astounded that she wanted to cook for herself, and had kept reiterating that there were world-class chefs on site who could whip up anything she desired—it nonetheless contained everything she needed.

Issy loved cooking. There were certain aromas, like freshly baked cakes and bread, that never failed to transport her back to a time when her family had been whole and happy. So far that day, she'd baked a lemon drizzle cake and made herself an Italian sausage pasta dish laden with parmesan. Comfort food. Instead of soothing her though, the aromas twisted her stomach to the extent that her plan to demolish the lot was foiled. It had been the same the day before, when she'd made profiteroles laden with whipped cream and chocolate and only managed to eat two of them.

If she was to believe Gianni's twisted accusation

against her father then that meant the happy memories she relied on to lift her spirits and make her believe that good times could once again come for her and Amelia and maybe even their mother were built on a lie. She couldn't believe her father had been corrupt. She just couldn't. Until the day the Rossi cousins had barged into their home and destroyed their lives, her father had been a kind and loving man who'd lavished all the love and time he could spare on his family. Would a corrupt man cut short a business meeting so he could watch his six-year-old daughter perform the challenging role of a snowflake in a ballet recital? Would a corrupt man make every effort to be home by his daughters' bedtimes each night so he could read to them?

And would her mother, a once fun-loving, sweet, kind, joyful woman marry a corrupt man? Absolutely not.

Gianni was lying to her. He had to be. Probably because he didn't want to have to confront the damage *his* thievery and corruption had caused, and the more she thought this, the greater her outrage grew. How dare he twist things to make her father the bad guy?

There was a knock on her cabin's front door.

Crossing the airy living area adorned with the most exquisite furniture to the door, she guardedly asked, 'Who is it?'

'Me.'

She pressed a hand to her chest to stop her suddenly thrashing heart from bursting out. 'Are you here to set me free?'

'You are free, *bella*. You can go wherever you like in the complex.'

'Am I free to leave the complex?'

'No.'

'Then go away.'

'You can't spend all your time in here. It's not good for you.'

'If I was to leave this chalet I guarantee it wouldn't be good for you.'

His laughter rumbled through the door and made her want to cover her ears. 'That's a risk I'm prepared to take. Come on, Issy, we could be here for a few more days. You can't spend it locked away. Come out and explore with me. We can talk.'

'In case you hadn't noticed, I don't want to talk to you, and I don't need to leave this cabin. You're a great host and there is plenty here to keep me occupied, so do me a favour and leave me alone. I'm not going anywhere until you let me go home.'

'You'll be free to go home as soon as I get word from Alessandro, but we will need to talk at some point.'

'We have nothing to say to each other.'

'We have a marriage to dissolve.'

'Then get dissolving it and leave me alone.'

Realising she was close to tears, Issy hurried back through the living area and out into her stunning private garden.

Gianni stared at Issy's chalet door. Still locked. Still no sighting of her. He regretted now making sure each chalet had all the privacy the occupants could wish for. These were the chalets for his close friends to use and for Alessandro, who he fully intended to one day drag here.

He knocked on the door. No answer came so he knocked again.

Her voice was even more guarded than it had been the day before. 'Yes?'

'It's me.'

She didn't respond at all.

'You can't avoid me for ever,' he said, and as he said it, he smiled ruefully to imagine her thinking, *Just you ruddy watch me.*

'Okay, you don't have to let me in,' he said after she'd ignored him for another twenty seconds, 'and I can't force you to talk to me. But I can sit here and talk to you and hope that you'll listen.'

Although the windows of the chalet were tinted to ensure complete privacy and her shutters closed so he couldn't see in, he sensed she was still at the door and hadn't rushed into the garden to escape his voice as she'd done the day before.

Lowering himself onto the front door step, he took a drink of the water he'd brought with him, made himself as comfortable as he could and rested his head back against the door.

'My father is a monster,' he said. 'A true monster. His brother—Alessandro's father—is the same. I don't know how they came to be that way, maybe their own father who I never met was the same, but their mother, our *nonna*, was a great lady. She lived with us and her presence tempered the worst of them. She died when I was eight.'

Gianni swallowed the acrid taste that had built in his mouth.

'Before she died, I was used to being hit. It was normal. Alessandro suffered the same. After she died the monsters came out. You know we were raised in Umbria?'

There was no answer but something told him she was listening.

He gave a morose laugh through his nose. 'I assume you know. I assume you know too that our fathers' business is wine. That's public knowledge for anyone who searches for it and I think you have searched my name and discovered everything the internet can tell you about me. If I were in your shoes and believed my father to be innocent then I would have done the same with the same intent, and I think that speaks of how different our childhoods were. If you were to tell me my father was innocent of something I would laugh in your face.'

Issy had tried to walk away from the door and out of the living area when Gianni had identified himself as her visitor but her feet had refused to obey. She'd tried to cover her ears when he'd started talking but her hands had refused to obey.

With a choked sigh of defeat, she slid her back down the door until her bottom reached the bamboo floor, then pulled her knees to her chest and hugged herself tightly.

'The wine they produce used to be great but when

their mother died, they started cutting corners wherever they could. When Alessandro and I left, they cut even more corners. I give them two more years before the vineyard stops producing. At the most.' He laughed. Issy imagined his throat extending. 'Now, they're too lazy to even fertilise their land properly and since we left, too mean to pay anyone else to do it for them. Add all the other corners they cut and it's no surprise their Sangiovese tastes like battery acid.'

A long silence followed before he continued, still speaking in the same even tone as if relating a story he'd heard many times. But this wasn't *a* story. This was *his* story. All the things she'd longed to know even though it had had no relevance to her quest. Issy had wanted to know for her own sake because as much as Gianni had repelled her, deep down in the place she'd never dared acknowledge to herself lived an aching fascination for him.

'We were their little slaves,' he said. 'I remember crushing grapes with my feet until midnight and going to school the next day with purple feet and ankles. We were forced to work from sunrise until they said stop. If we complained, we were hit. Once Nonna died, we didn't have to complain to be hit. Her death unleashed them. They were our true slave masters and we their punching bags. Our mothers too. They never needed an excuse to beat them.'

Issy covered her mouth to stop a moan of distress escaping. She thought of the bump in Gianni's nose and how she'd wanted to shake the hand of the person who'd done it. That person must have been his own father.

'My mother ran away a year after Nonna died.' For the first time she heard an inflection of emotion in his voice. 'I haven't seen her since. She lives in Milan. I pay money into her account each month, but I never see her. She abandoned me to that bastard. It took months before I accepted that she wasn't coming back for me.' The tinge of sadness that laced his next laugh made her insides contract. 'My mother left me to my fate. Andro and I made a pact when we were twelve that as soon as we'd both turned eighteen we would leave and build new lives for ourselves. We worked even harder, taking jobs outside the vineyard wherever we could and saving every cent our fathers didn't demand we hand over to them. My father never knew, but I left school at sixteen and got a full-time job at a pizzeria—he'd have only taken my wages from me. The first thing we did when we finally left the vineyard was change our surnames.'

Vizzini, she remembered. That had been his original surname. It had taken her ages to dig that up. She remembered thinking Rossi suited him better and then had chided herself for thinking such a thing. Who cared whether his name suited him?

'We chose our *nonna*'s surname,' he said quietly, and though she had no way of knowing, Issy was certain he knew she was sat on the other side of the door to him. 'We sorted all the legal side out and then we made an offer on Tuscan land we'd huge plans for. We hadn't saved enough money to purchase it outright but we were able to borrow the shortfall.'

Dread crept its way up from the pit of her stomach.

'Only after the land was paid for and transferred into our names did we learn it was unstable. There was no possibility of building a housing development on it. We'd been conned. The seller had seen two fresh-faced eighteen-year-olds and took advantage of our naivety. He bribed the surveyor and everyone else involved in the transaction and left us staring at bankruptcy.'

The seller. The man he claimed was her father.

'He underestimated us,' he said simply. 'We'd worked too hard and overcome too much to accept defeat. We started again. We worked like Trojans to repay the loan and build a new nest. As soon as we had the money we bought our first property and flipped it; gave it a makeover and sold it for a profit. We brought our second property and then our third and then we set our sights further taking on bigger and bigger projects with proportionate profits until we had the money to force the takeover of the business of the man who'd ripped us off. It took us four years. I don't think either of us slept more than four hours a night in those days. I do not regret what we did to that man. It didn't take much detective work to discover we weren't his only victims. I cannot abide corruption, Issy, and I hope that one day soon you will tell me of this proof of corruption Amelia spoke of because I swear on Alessandro's life that we are not corrupt. Everything we have we've built with our own toil using our own blood and sweat.'

Gianni's backside had become numb. Issy hadn't made a single sound but he was certain she'd heard every word. He rolled his neck and got to his feet. 'I'm going for a swim. Dinner will be served in the open dining room of my lodge at seven. All you need do is follow the path facing the beach and it will lead you to it. There is no pressure but know I would be glad to see you. I don't like to think of you alone with your thoughts…' He exhaled slowly before admitting, 'I want to get to know the real Isabelle Seymore because I already miss the Issy I spent that ride wild on the *Palazzo delle Feste* with. I know she's not the real you, but something tells me the things I like the most about her *are* real.'

Issy tried desperately hard to concentrate on the game of solitaire she was playing but her eyes kept being drawn to her watch. Gianni would be in his dining room, but he wouldn't be waiting for her. She'd left word for him declining his invitation when she'd requested dinner be brought to her cabin.

She couldn't face her stomach turning over at the aromas of her own cooking and she couldn't face him. It was too dangerous. She'd listened to Gianni relay the story of his life and wanted so much to open the door, crawl onto his lap and hold him tight. She'd long suspected his estrangement from his father was rooted in something bad—children rarely cut themselves off from their parents without good reason—but to imagine the suffering he must have gone through…

As hard as she tried to keep her emotions contained, the stone wall she'd built was breaking down, the contents of her heart bleeding out of it.

But there were three villains to his story. His father, his uncle and her father.

She couldn't accept it. Her bleeding heart wouldn't accept it. Her father would never treat two young men the way Gianni had described. He just wouldn't.

Are you sure...?

She slammed a card down then grabbed a chip. They were the most delicious chips she'd ever eaten in her life and she wished she wasn't feeling so down while eating them. She should be savouring their deliciousness.

Gianni must have been mistaken about her father. Because that was the crux of the problem—she believed him. Believed that he believed it.

And what about her sister? Because if Gianni was speaking the truth then it meant Amelia, the anchor that had kept Issy afloat all these years, had lied to her.

Mid-morning the next day, Gianni knocked on Issy's door again.

This time there was more hesitancy than guardedness in her voice. 'Yes?'

'It's me.'

Silence.

'I missed you last night.'

A long beat passed. 'Did you get my message?'

'I did.' He hadn't expected her to come. He'd hoped but his gut had told him not to hope too hard. He couldn't understand why her message, when it had come, had still landed like a blow.

There were many things about his reactions to Issy that Gianni didn't understand. Reactions and feelings he'd never felt before. They were growing stronger.

The need to seek her out even if only to hear her voice gaining strength.

'Ready to come out yet?' he asked.

There was a slight hesitation before she said, 'No. Not yet.'

Not yet? That was a huge improvement and his chest lightened to hear it. 'That's a shame. It's a beautiful day.'

'I know. I've been in the garden.'

'Swimming?'

He swore he heard her laugh. 'No. I don't think it's safe for me to swim without a lifeguard close to hand.'

'That's one less thing for me to worry about,' he joked back. He resisted offering to be her lifeguard. One step at a time. After days of silence and her cold shoulder, her voice sounded markedly warmer. Softer. 'Have you always been a lousy swimmer?'

'No… I… It's just been a long time. That's all. And I was never that strong a swimmer.'

He sat down in the same spot as he'd taken the day before. 'Tell me about it.'

'About what?'

'Swimming. Your life. Anything you want to tell me.'

'What do you want to know?' she asked doubtfully.

'Everything.'

When she next spoke her voice sounded so close to his ear that he knew she'd sat down too and that her back was likely pressed against the door the same as his, like two bookends. 'Be more specific.'

He wondered if her head touched the door too. She

was so much shorter than him that it would rest lower than his. He wondered, too, why he'd always been inclined towards tall women before Issy. 'Tell me about your job. You're a nurse?'

'I'm an auxiliary nurse, not a medical nurse.'

'Is there a difference?'

'About four years of education.' Another quip? Things really were improving. He heard the smile in her voice as she explained, 'My job is basically to make sure the patients are comfortable and to help them with anything they can't do for themselves.'

'You work with children?'

'Yes. I'm on the children's ward.'

'You enjoy it?'

'I love it.'

'Is it not hard dealing with sick children?'

'It can be. You have to stay professional but it's hard not to build attachments. Especially with the really sick ones.'

'The ones you know will die?'

Her next, 'Yes,' was barely audible through the barrier of the door.

Her voice lifted a little. 'But they're incredible. All of them. Children are so brave, much braver than adults.'

'Do you really think that?'

'That's just from my observations over the last four years.'

'I know very little about children,' he mused. 'I've never been in a social setting with a child.'

'Never?'

'Never,' he confirmed. 'I've never held a baby either.'

'You've missed out.'

'How?'

He imagined the shrug she gave at this. 'Holding a baby is the most contenting thing in the world.'

'You want children of your own?'

'Definitely.' She paused before adding, 'You?'

'I've never thought about it until this minute, but I think I would like children. With the right woman.' The image of a small, plump, chestnut-haired Issy holding an ice cream sundae flashed in his mind. Immediately disconcerted, he blinked the image away and moved the subject away from children. 'Did you never want to be a real nurse?'

'Nursing was founded on caring for the sick and that's what I do, but originally I wanted to be a medical nurse.'

'What stopped you?'

There was another long beat before she softly answered, 'You.'

He closed his eyes and filled his lungs with air. 'Tell me, *bella*. Tell me everything.'

She took so long to speak he became convinced that she'd slipped away. 'When our father lost the business it had a domino effect on the rest of our lives. Looking back, it feels like it happened overnight, but I must have been sleepwalking through it. One minute I was the luckiest girl alive, living in a big, beautiful house in London and spending my summers in our home in Italy. I went to a school I loved, I had great friends, a loving family... The next minute it was all gone. We lost our home. Amelia and I were forced to leave our school—our parents couldn't afford the fees—and start again at a new one where the other students hated us. Most of our friends abandoned us and our parents' friends abandoned them too. Dad always liked a drink, but I don't remember ever seeing him drunk before, but from that day I don't have a single memory of him sober. A year later he was dead. He literally drank himself to death.'

Gianni rubbed his temples. He remembered hearing on the grapevine about Thomas Seymore's death. The grapevine had whispered about alcohol. For once it seemed the grapevine had been correct.

'After his death, Mum was forced to file for bankruptcy and we were forced to move again—we'd become so poor the council had to provide us with accommodation. I think, though I don't know for certain, that that's when her drug dependency started. Amelia clocked on to it before I did—she's always been more observant than me—and protected me from it as much as she could but she couldn't protect me for ever. I just know that when I lost my dad, the last of the mother that lived in the woman that is Jane Seymore died with him.'

'She really is addicted to drugs?'

'Yes. We looked after her as best we could, but we were kids. As soon as Lia got the job with you, we could afford to send her to rehab in South America. Lia found it. Mum likes it there…as much as she likes being anywhere on this earth.'

A long passage of silence passed before she said,

'Everything we went through pulled me and Amelia together. Her strength was amazing and, in a way, inspired me to be strong too. She kept me sane. We took care of Mum and each other, and we vowed revenge on the men we believed killed our father and drove our mother into addiction. We wanted to hit you where it hurt and that meant your business. Every single thing we've done since Amelia went to university to get the qualifications that would make her the ideal candidate for your company has been with that end goal.'

'You've played the support act?'

'No. I was the backroom worker in the project but we've supported each other. Every decision we made together. All the money we earned went into the same pot.'

'But you wanted to be a medical nurse.'

'I needed to be earning money. Believe me, we both made sacrifices but neither of us saw it as that, and it worked out for the best. I love my job and being so hands on with the kids. It's the most rewarding job in the world and I wouldn't change it for anything.'

The ache that formed in Gianni's chest at this was so acute that he had to exhale slowly to relieve it. 'A few times just then when you were speaking of your revenge, you spoke in the past tense...' He was, absurdly, almost afraid to ask. 'Does that mean you believe me?'

CHAPTER TWELVE

Issy BOWED HER head and breathed deeply before leaning back against the door and dragging her hair off her face. 'I don't... Gianni, please...' She pinched the bridge of her nose and fought back the hot swell of tears. 'I've... I've had some doubts.'

'What kind of doubts?' he asked gently.

Bitter-tasting guilt rose up her throat at what she was about to admit. 'We took everything he said in blind faith.'

'I know it hurts, *bella*, but admitting that he was a bastard in business does not have to taint your memories of who he was as your father.'

'But I feel disloyal for even questioning it to myself,' she whispered.

'A child is programmed to trust their parents,' he said in that same gentle tone. 'When my mother ran away without me... It came close to breaking me. My own mother abandoned me and I've never been able to trust anyone but Alessandro since.'

Not wanting to inadvertently offend him, Issy hesitated before asking, 'Is that why you've never had a long-term relationship?'

He gave a low laugh. 'I never think about it but that's very likely. My social life is great fun and I have many friends, but no one I would consider close. That includes my past lovers. I've never had a conversation like this with anyone before or shared the confidences I did with you yesterday.'

'It's the same for me,' she admitted. 'I've always had Amelia to talk to and we confide absolutely everything in each other, but I think that's because we *had* to pull together. If she hadn't been there I think I would have grown to hate my parents for sinking into dependency, you know, for not being enough to keep them sober. I always make myself remember how it was before the business was taken and how happy we were as a family and how secure I felt—I *have* to hold on to that. When I FaceTime my mum, I sometimes catch glimpses of the mum I remember and I cherish those moments, and when I think of my dad I remember the man who read to me and led all the standing ovations at my ballet recitals, and it kills me to think that wasn't who he really was.'

'That *is* who he was, *cara*. The family man and the businessman were separate parts of him.'

'But if he sold you that land fraudulently and bribed officials to make it happen then his protestations of innocence after you forced the takeover were lies, and if you're right that there were other victims then that means my entire childhood is tainted.'

'Only if you let it be tainted.'

'But it means everything we had, all the privileges Amelia and I enjoyed, were built on fraud and lies.'

'But the father he was to you wasn't a lie. He loved you and Amelia and it seems to me that he destroyed himself in alcohol because he couldn't live with the repercussions of what his business decisions had done to his family.'

'I can't believe you're sticking up for him.' Not after everything. How could Gianni give her reassurance after what she'd tried to do to him?

'He must have had some good in him to produce a daughter like you.'

'What, a vengeful liar who was hell-bent on destroying you?'

'No, a fiercely loyal, kind-hearted, beautiful woman who couldn't go through with her vengeance without additional evidence. Don't forget, I have read the messages between you and your sister. When she messaged you that she'd found proof of corruption against us, your reply said, Thank God for that. That same day you took a photo of yourself with a patient and your hair was still chestnut. In the few days between that message and photo being taken to when we met in the club, you'd dyed your hair. You had doubts, *cara*, I know you did, and your sister knew it too and told you what you needed to hear to get you to actually act on your plans.'

The tears Issy had been holding back fell down her cheeks. How could a man she'd known for such a short time have the power to decipher her own thoughts and feelings better than she was able to?

'*Bella?*'

Breathing deeply, she wiped her eyes on her knees. 'I can't believe I'm admitting this but you're right, I've had doubts about his version of what happened between you and him.' Doubts that had grown the deeper she'd delved into Gianni's life and found nothing remotely untoward about his business conduct, doubts compounded with every gushing interview and profile published about him. No one had a bad word to say about him, not even his broken-hearted lovers. 'But, Gianni, I don't have any doubts about Amelia. None at all. She's my rock and guardian angel rolled into one. I can't bear to think of what would have happened to me without her. Why would she lie to me? *Why?*'

Now he was the one to take his time to answer, saying slowly, 'I can't answer that but you need to think on this—why did she message such important news to you instead of calling you? Your whole plan hinged on Amelia finding proof that we were corrupt to push you into action. Consider if it is possible she messaged instead of calling because she was afraid you'd hear the lie in her voice.'

Issy sat on the edge of her private swimming pool with her legs submerged in the warm water up to mid-calf. Soon, the sun would make its descent and fill the sky with the orange haze that had captured her attention every night she'd stayed on this island. It had been her only respite from thinking of Gianni.

She was still thinking of him.

Gianni Rossi had occupied much of her thoughts in

the years since she and Amelia had first hatched their plan. At the start of it all, it had been a tiny flightless fledgling plan but over the years it had grown in substance. Grown wings. As the plan had developed and she'd begun her research on him, slowly but surely Gianni had begun to occupy more headspace. By the time she'd started her job at the hospital he was the first thing she thought of when she woke and the last image she saw before she fell asleep.

She would never know the truth of what happened between Gianni, Alessandro and her father but she accepted that whatever Gianni had done, he truly believed her father had fleeced him. She did believe that. Gianni was not the monster she'd believed for so long; a belief she'd had to keep feeding to herself over the years to stop from faltering in her quest.

Amelia had sensed Issy's doubts. She was certain of it.

She closed her eyes and pressed her hand to her belly to ride the spasm of guilt that came from her own doubts. She couldn't think of Amelia right now, couldn't bear to let her mind take her where it so desperately didn't want to go.

Her eyes snapped back open. What she wanted was Gianni. To feel the light that always filled her when his gaze captured hers. To go to him as Isabelle Seymore, the auxiliary nurse who liked ballet, books and junk food more than was good for her, both of them stripped back to just their essences, all pretence and deception between them gone.

And she wanted to know the real Gianni, the man

who'd opened up to her and without an ounce of self-pity told her his story.

She had a strong feeling that all the things she'd been helpless to stop herself from liking about him were the real Gianni.

No more thinking about the past.

Gianni sat at the end of the twenty-foot dining table laid for two, as it had been on board his yacht that night, and had a large drink of cold white wine.

Would she come?

He hadn't felt this nervous since his first date all those years ago.

He'd invited Issy to share dinner with him. Again. She hadn't given him an answer. Again. But her silence had been different this time. Allowed a sliver of hope to settle in him.

She hadn't left a polite message declining. Yet. He looked at his watch and popped a large green olive in his mouth. There was still time for her to back out… not that she'd actually said yes.

Hope was dangerous, he rued, now reaching for a breadstick and forcing his gaze on the spectacular sunset unfolding before him rather than keeping it fixed on the path she would join him from. If she came.

How had this happened? Going from a potential fling to a seductive game with a hustler, to learning the truth about her, to this? All along this was supposed to have been nothing but fun, the same as all his other flings but with added bite.

He'd never imagined he would feel like this, that he *could* feel like this. Like he was losing his head.

The hairs on the back of his neck rose. His heart thumped.

He whipped his head to the left before his brain caught up with what his senses were telling him.

Emerging from the darkening shadows of the foliage-lined path, her eyes locked on his face, was Issy.

The closer she moved towards him the harder his heart pumped. Dressed in a pretty pale yellow sundress with the spaghetti straps she favoured but which caressed her body with a swing around the knees rather than constricted it, barely a scrap of make-up graced her face. It had no need of it. Her silky blonde hair hung loose, sweeping over her shoulders, the first real hint of chestnut that had so captivated him in her photos emerging at the roots, the two colours blending together to create something uniquely beautiful.

Unable to tear her gaze from Gianni's face, Issy climbed the three steps onto the podium that served as his outside dining room. In the periphery of her vision silver fairy lights twinkled the perimeter of the wooden roof, a row of night-lights flickering on the table. With the sound of the sea lapping on the beach behind her, the whole scene was so dreamily romantic her whole being felt consumed by it.

But it was the man in the crisp white open-necked shirt and smart dark grey shorts who'd risen to his feet and taken slow steps towards her who consumed her the most. To see the way his chest was rising and falling as if it had a weight in it and the expression in the eyes as rooted to hers as hers were to his, an expression that was more, much more, than hunger…

Standing before him, she raised her arm and palmed his cheek. The thick stubble from four days ago had grown into a fully fledged beard. The pads of her fingers tingled madly in reaction to the sharp yet soft texture and her longing for him intensified.

His nostrils flared. His strong throat moved.

The tiny gap between them closed. His hands skimmed her waist then tightened around it.

Without a single word being uttered, he lifted her into air. Her face hovering above his, her hair brushing against his face, he continued to stare at her as if she were a miracle come to life before lowering her gently and then sweeping her into his arms so she was cradled against his chest.

Nestling her cheek against his beating heart, Issy breathed him in. The freshness of his cologne mingled with his clean skin enveloped her open senses. Open because she would no longer close any of herself off to him.

Gianni carried Issy up the stairs to his bedroom. She fit perfectly in his arms.

Gently, he sat her at the foot of the bed. Her eyes were open. Trusting. She reached a hand out to him. Capturing it, he kissed her pretty fingers, then stepped back to strip his clothes. First came the shirt which he shrugged over his head and let drop wherever it landed. Next came his shorts. He unbuttoned them and tugged the zip down, then, pinching his snug boxers with them, pulled them down his hips and thighs until gravity took care of the rest. Stepping out of them, he kicked his deck shoes off and had to force air into his lungs at the expression on Issy's face as she drank him in… Because that's how it felt. As if she were drinking in every part of him.

For the first time in his entire life, Gianni felt stripped to his marrow.

He took a step to close the small gap between them but she shook her head softly to stop him and got to her feet.

His heart had swollen so hard it came close to choking him. He watched as she pulled the dress up her beautiful body and over her head. Just as he'd done, she gave no care to where it landed.

Her hands went around her back. A moment later her pretty white silk bra fell the same way as her dress and all that was left were the matching panties. Clasping them with the tips of her fingers, she pinched the sides and pulled them down until she was able to step out of them. And then she straightened, cheeks flush, barely breathing, and it was his turn to drink *her* in.

During their time on the *Palazzo delle Feste*, Gianni had feasted his eyes on her for hours and hours. It felt like he was looking at her anew. Slowly, he soaked in every inch of her, from the tiny brown mole on the side of her neck to the small, pert breasts with their beautiful dusky pink nipples to the neat triangle of dark brown hair between her legs all the way down to her painted toes.

Head tilted back, eyes wide on his, she took the step to him. His arousal jutted into the base of her belly.

Her lips parted, a small breath pulled in. Her eyes darkened and pulsed.

Slowly, he ran his hands down her bare arms. *'Tu sei bella...'* he whispered hoarsely.

Her chest rose, her voice barely audible as she whispered back, *'Anche tu.'*

So are you...

He lifted her back into his arms. Her arms locked around his neck. Carrying her around the bed, he laid her down so her head rested on a pillow. Her hair spilled around her like a fan.

He didn't know what ached the most, his heart or his arousal.

He had never felt like this. Never felt such need for someone that his whole body trembled at the strength of it.

Issy felt like she'd been transported into the fairy lights that had barely penetrated her consciousness before Gianni swept her into his arms, a magical dreamlike reality filled entirely with him. When he laid himself on top of her, resting his weight on his elbows either side of her head so as not to crush her, the tips of her breasts pressed against the hardness of his chest, she would swear she felt the strength of his heartbeat as clearly as she felt her own.

The wonder in his stare as he lowered his face to hers made her heart beat even faster, and when his lips finally captured hers, flames ignited in it, pumping fire through her veins and melting the last of her thoughts.

Closing her eyes, she sank into the wonder that was

Gianni and the tenderness underlying the passion of his kisses.

His mouth and hands explored her with a reverence that left her molten. Barely an inch of her flesh went untouched, unkissed, unloved. When he trailed his tongue up her inner thigh and pressed it against her swollen nub, every nerve ending in her body responded and she was helpless to do anything but cry his name and ride the thrills of the climax he slowly brought her to.

Dazed, drugged on bliss, she pulled herself up as Gianni raised his head. This time she was the one to kiss him. This time she was the one to lay him down and worship every inch of the body of the man who had captivated her for so long.

With the taste of Issy's climax still on his tongue, Gianni submitted to an assault of his senses that would have lost him his mind if it wasn't already gone. Every touch and mark of her mouth and tongue scorched him. Never had he been on the receiving end of such pleasure, but it was much more than that, more than a bodily experience, this transcended *everything...*

He groaned and had to grit his teeth when she took hold of his erection, then grit them even harder when she took him in her mouth.

Mio Dio...

He looked down and her gaze lifted to his. His heart punched through him to see the desire-laden wonder in her stare.

Closing his eyes, he gathered her hair lightly and let her take the lead, throwing his head back as her movements, tentative at first, became emboldened. The fist she'd made around the base tightened and she took him deeper into her mouth, moaning her own pleasure at the pleasure she was giving him.

If heaven existed he'd just found it.

Mio Dio, this was like nothing…*nothing*…

The tell-tale tug of his orgasm began to pull at him, and with an exhale of air, he gently pulled away from her.

Her gaze lifted to him again, a tiny knot of confusion on her brow.

Throat too constricted to speak, he cupped her cheeks and kissed her deeply, pushing her onto her back and sliding himself between her legs with the motion.

The tip of his erection brushed against her opening, the urge to just bury himself inside her with one long thrust so strong he had to clamp his jaw and squeeze his eyes shut to stop his basest instincts from taking him over.

Issy was a virgin. They needed protection.

The burning desire to say to hell with the consequence of no protection…

Keeping himself positioned between her legs, he stretched his arm out. No sooner had he tugged open the drawer of his bedside table than Issy lifted her head and began open-mouth kissing his neck while dragging a hand down his chest and abdomen to take hold of his erection.

Dear God in heaven…

He groped and fumbled for a condom; fumbled because she was masturbating him and deepening the French kisses on his neck.

The foil open, he removed the condom and took the hand Issy was giving him such glorious pleasure with. Her mouth moved up to his jaw until she found his lips, and, somehow, tongues fused and their hands clasped together, they rolled the condom on. Barely a second passed before she was flat on her back again, short, jagged breaths coming from her mouth, her eyes boring into his, his erection jutting and straining against her heat.

Issy felt possessed, that there was every chance she would go insane if Gianni didn't take possession of her. She had never wanted anything as badly as she wanted this. Every inch of her body was alight with the flames he'd ignited, her senses consumed with him. His beautiful face was all she could see, his ragged breaths all she could hear, his musky skin all she could smell and all she could taste, the smoothness of his skin all she could feel.

His lips grazed hers lightly and then he began to press his way inside her.

There was no pain, no discomfort, just a slow-building sensation of being deliciously filled and stretched until their groins locked together and they were as one.

Gianni thought he'd found heaven when Issy had taken him into her mouth. If that was heaven then this was paradise, a miracle of the flesh and soul.

They could just stay like this, he thought dimly. Fused together. As one.

Never had the need for release burned so deeply but

the urgency had gone. Now all he wanted was to savour this moment, savour Issy…

Issy had thought she'd already experienced all the sensual pleasure there was to feel but when Gianni began to move inside her, a whole new feeling grew, the burn in her core deepening and then uncoiling like tendrils through her very being.

Hooking a hand to his neck, she kissed him and closed her eyes.

Slowly, slowly, his thrusts lengthened and deepened. Slowly, slowly, the incredible pleasure increased until she was nothing but a mass of nerve endings and the burning pressure deep inside of her exploded.

With a long cry, she buried her mouth into his neck and held tight as rolling waves of bliss flooded her. Somewhere in the recess of her mind, she heard Gianni groan loudly, and then there was one last furious thrust that locked their groins together for one final time.

Buried as deep inside Issy as he'd ever dreamed it was possible to be, Gianni's climax roared through him. And still he tried to bury deeper, still she tried to pull him deeper, both of them desperately drawing out the pleasure for as long as they could until there was nothing left but stunned silence.

CHAPTER THIRTEEN

GIANNI STARED AT the sleeping face turned to his and smiled to see the light smattering of freckles highlighted on Issy's nose and cheeks by the early morning sunlight streaming in.

The temptation to wake her was strong but his conscience would not allow him. She must be exhausted. Three days and four nights of almost constant lovemaking had left her with faint bruises under her eyes. As for him… Despite the lack of sleep, Gianni felt the best he'd felt in so long that he couldn't remember when he'd ever felt this good. This alive.

Carefully rolling onto his back, he stretched an arm above his head.

'Morning.'

He turned his head. Issy's eyes had opened, a sleepy smile playing on her lips.

He leaned his face to hers and brushed a kiss to her lips. Her smile widened.

'It's early,' he said quietly. 'Go back to sleep.'

She nudged herself closer to him and placed a hand on his chest. 'I don't want to sleep.'

Taking her hand, he took a long breath knowing exactly what she meant. The four days they'd spent as lovers had passed almost like a dream. It had been just them. Gianni's room covered the whole second floor, a sprawling open-plan space with his hand-crafted emperor bed, a small dining table, a large corner sofa with accompanying entertainment centre, a bar, a walk-in wardrobe and en suite. They'd eaten in this room food brought to them by staff who left it at the door, drank from his bar which was topped up the few times they'd escaped to his private pool. It was as if they were the only two people in the whole world.

He raised his head at the sound of rustling and saw a note being pushed under the door.

Kissing Issy first, he climbed out of bed for it. As he opened it, he looked at her. She'd thrown the bedsheets off and struck such a provocative pose that he almost threw the note away unread. Almost.

The message was from Alessandro, four words: The business is safe.

That was it. No other information.

He read it again and waited to feel something lift in him.

Something didn't come.

Why wasn't he ecstatic? For sure, he'd known Alessandro would fix things. He'd never doubted that. But he'd expected to at least feel relief, not an immediate plummet of dread in his stomach.

'What's wrong?' she asked softly.

He met her stare. For a long moment he debated

whether or not to tell her. 'Alessandro has sorted everything.'

'With the business?'

'Yes.'

'Oh.'

He had to swallow to make his throat move but before he could speak, she said, 'I'm glad.'

'You are?'

To his horror, tears filled her eyes. She nodded. 'I'm sorry for what we tried to do to you. Really sorry.'

His lungs compressed. 'I know you are.'

'Please forgive me.'

Sitting on the bed, he brushed away the tear that rolled down her cheek. 'It's already forgiven.'

Issy tried desperately hard to stop any more tears from leaking. She didn't want to cry in front of him but reality had just inserted itself into the dream of their life. She'd refused to think of anything but Gianni since they'd become lovers. It had been the same for him too, she was certain. It had been the two of them in a private, dreamy bubble. When not making love they'd spoken about so many things, had long, laughter-filled discussions about their lives and interests, getting to know each other as who they really were, but by unspoken agreement there had been no mention of his cousin or business—other than generically—or her sister or parents. What they'd found together was too special, too *magical*, to allow the things that meant it had to come to an end spoil it for the time they had.

He wiped another tear. 'You are free to go home now.'

But that only made her want to cry harder. 'Do you want me to go?'

He shook his head with vehemence. 'No.'

'Good,' she said in a whisper. 'Because I don't want to go either.'

He closed his eyes as if in relief, his shoulders rising before he locked them back on hers. 'Your phone is in my dressing room.'

That made her smile. 'I'd forgotten all about it.'

'You can call your sister.'

But there was a reason Issy hadn't allowed herself to think of her sister let alone talk about her. 'You said she was safe.'

'She is.'

'Then I don't need to call her. Not yet.'

From the way Gianni's eyes were searching hers, she had the feeling he knew exactly how torn she was about Amelia.

Wrapping her arms around his neck, she pulled him down for a heady, passion-filled kiss.

The man who made her feel so, so much didn't have to return to his real life for another four of five days... oh, hell, she was losing track of time...and she would extract every ounce of the pleasure and joy being with him brought her until their time ran out.

Reality could wait a while longer.

The sea was much warmer than Issy anticipated, and she didn't even flinch when it reached the top of her legs. When it reached her bellybutton, she stopped. 'This is as far as I go,' she declared.

'Wimp,' Gianni teased with that smile that never failed to make her heart go all squidgy.

'I am not a wimp!'

He threw the beach ball at her. 'Yes, you are.'

She caught it and threw it back. 'No, I'm not.'

His grin widened. 'How am I supposed to pull you under if you won't go any further than your stomach?'

'You want me to drown?' she asked in mock outrage.

'No.' He lobbed the ball hard at her. 'I want to save you from drowning so I can give you the kiss of life.'

'You need one of those banana float things if you're going to act as lifeguard again,' she reminded him.

'I can't wait to unwrap it on my birthday.

'I'll need to use a whole tree's worth of wrapping paper,' she said, and used all her strength to chuck the ball at him and laughed with glee when her aim finally came good and the ball bounced off his head.

'You did that on purpose!' he accused, scooping the ball up and tucking it under his arm.

'I don't know what you're talking about.'

He strode through the water towards her. 'You have an evil streak in you.'

Giggling, she waded backwards, trying to escape him. 'Only when it comes to beach balls.'

He held the ball above his head, eyes gleaming as he loomed down on her. Having such long legs and only being thigh-high in the water meant he'd closed the gap far quicker than she'd been able to flee. But instead of dropping the ball on her head, he threw it aside and then, with a speed and grace that had no place on a man of his size, lifted her by the waist and threw her in the air.

She landed backside first with a squeal, kicking feet and flailing arms submerging at the same time as her face went under. Rising back to the surface, trying her hardest not to laugh, a task made harder by the throaty, uproarious sounds coming out of Gianni's mouth, she half crawled to him and grabbed his calves.

'You think you can knock me over?' he mocked, and in a flash he had her by the waist again and for the second time in less than two minutes, Issy was flying in the air and landing with a splash. When she resurfaced, the ball was in reach. Grabbing it, she threw it at him and got him on the forehead.

'Oh, that does it,' he said with a shake of his head, now wading towards her like a panther on the prowl.

By now breast height in the water, Issy, cackling with laughter, tried to swim away from him. She'd barely managed three strokes when he captured an ankle and pulled her under. She came up for air with a splutter, only to be bodily lifted from the sea by a single arm wrapped around her waist and carried to the beach.

Laughing too hard to scream or pretend any form of protest, the most she could do was slap feebly at his shoulders when he laid her down on the sand.

'I just saved your life!' he admonished sternly, which only made the absurdity of it all funnier. 'Now stop laughing so I can give you the kiss of life.'

Clamping her lips together so stop any more giggles coming out, Issy immediately played dead.

The expected kiss took much longer to press against

her expectant lips than she'd anticipated. She peered through one eye to see what the hold-up was and found Gianni gazing down at her with an expression in his eyes that made her heart clench. Breaking character, she pressed a hand to his cheek and rubbed her palm against his beard. He captured the hand and kissed it reverently. 'You're beautiful, did you know that?'

Her chest filled with an emotion she didn't understand but which was thick enough to cramp her lungs. 'You make me feel beautiful,' she whispered.

'You are beautiful, Isabelle, and I want you to promise me you will never starve yourself again.'

She thought of the meals they'd shared these last six days, how happiness and wonderful sex had increased her appetite, how her bikinis—literally the only clothing she'd worn since they'd become lovers—were already feeling tight at the hips. The emotions filling her swelled even more. 'I starved myself to entrap you.'

He kissed her hand again. 'I'd already guessed that. And I can guess why you felt you needed to do that and to dye your beautiful hair.' He shook his head tightly. 'None of those women were real to me, Issy.'

'What do you mean?'

Gianni took a breath and tried to collate his thoughts. 'They were status symbols, like my penthouses, the watches I wear, the cars I drive or have driven for me. A way for me to flaunt the man I'd become to my father.'

She just stared at him.

'I've not seen him since we left Umbria,' he explained quietly. 'I never want to see him again.'

She threaded her fingers into his and squeezed.

'We knew, Alessandro and I, that changing our surname from theirs would hit them where it hurt the hardest.'

'Their egos?' she guessed.

He smiled at her astuteness. 'I know it must kill my father to see my success and know his place in my history has been severed. I wanted him to see me with the best of everything the world has to offer and not even be able to take credit for my name.'

'And the best of everything included women?'

'Yes,' he agreed unflinchingly. It was only now, speaking it aloud, that Gianni understood how shallow and, yes, misogynistic his attitude to the women in his personal life had been. 'If I had passed you as you were two years ago in a street I would never have looked twice at you. I wanted what I believed was the male dream; the killer supermodel on my arm and in my bed.'

He deserved the hurt and distaste curling Issy's mouth, and gently tightened his hold on her hand to stop her pulling it away.

'I need to be honest with you,' he said. 'I have to be. After the way we started and all the lies, I don't ever want deception of any kind to come between us.'

Her eyes flickered.

'I wouldn't have looked twice at you because I'd trained myself only to see tall, blonde, obviously rich women,' he continued. 'I didn't need to see anything more than that because I wasn't looking for more. I had no interest in anything real.' He managed a smile and kissed her clasped hand. 'It's all this time with you, Issy, the way you make me feel… I didn't stand a chance. And being with you, the uniqueness of how we came to be; it has brought the past back to me in a way it hasn't been in a long, long time. I think of my mother now, alone in her Milanese flat and for the first time in over two decades, I don't hate her for not coming back to me.'

'Maybe she couldn't,' Issy suggested quietly. There was something about Gianni's tone and the way he was looking at her that made her heart thump. For the first time in what felt like for ever, there was dread in the beats.

He grimaced and shook his head. 'She could. The first place she fled to was a woman's shelter. I know this because my aunt told me. The people there would have helped her but she chose not to tell them about me.'

A whimper crawled out of her throat.

The grimace turned into a smile. 'Don't be sad for me, *cara*. It is thanks to you that I can now confront my past in a way I never let myself before—I *have* to confront it. I don't want it to have power over me any more. My mother left me because she didn't love me enough to take me with her. That is the crux of it.'

'I don't believe that,' she whispered vehemently. How could any woman on this earth fail to love Gianni, let alone the woman who'd given birth to him?

He brushed a finger against her cheek. 'I think my father beat the love out of her. She has never remarried or taken a lover. She doesn't even have friends.

That used to make me happy but now…' His chest rose then fell with flump. '*Bella*, your mother abandoned you too in her own way, but you don't hold any anger or bitterness towards her. Instead, you try to understand and help her. You forgive her. And that is what I must do. Forgive my mother for the hand life dealt her and trust that her abandonment was not my fault.' His eyes held hers. 'And trust that it doesn't have to affect the rest of my life.'

The dread that had been building in the thumps of Issy's heart were now so loud they almost deafened her. Instinct was screaming at her to change the subject now, right now, another, stronger part yearning to wrap her arms around him and hold him tight and swear that he could put his trust in her, that she would never let him down, that she would always be there for him. That she would never leave him.

But those words would be a lie. There was no future for them to place his trust in her, not in the way she sensed he'd been driving this conversation towards. In a few days they would go their separate ways. They would leave each other. That's how it had to be, and she stared at him, pleading with her eyes for him to understand, silently begging him not to say the words that would force her to hurt him, hurt them both.

Just two weeks ago Issy would never have believed she or any woman would have the power to hurt Gianni Rossi. But then, two weeks ago, she'd never believed he would have the power to hurt her. She'd thought herself immune to him. She'd been too stupid to see that she was already half in love with him.

His lips parted.

No! She wanted to scream. *Please, don't.*

'I love you, Issy,' he said quietly. Sincerely. Breaking her heart. 'I love you. I know our marriage was a game of bluff we both told ourselves we'd lost but…'

She scrambled up and onto her bottom and shook her head frantically. 'Please, Gio, don't.'

He blinked as if something had flown into his eye.

'Don't say it,' she begged. 'It can never be. You must know that.'

He stared at her for the longest time, fingers still tight around hers, a contortion of emotions flickering on his face. 'Tell me you don't love me.'

'Don't do this.'

'Tell me you don't love me.'

'Please.'

'Tell me you don't love me and I will end this conversation and seek an annulment as soon as we return to the mainland. All you have to do is say the words.'

'I don't l…' But her tongue refused to cooperate. Refused to tell the lie. Finally snatching her hand free from his she buried her face in her knees and cried, 'I *can't.*'

Gianni made himself breathe through the sharpness in his chest. Issy's inability to refute her love didn't ease the tension tightening throughout him. 'You do love me, *bella,*' he said steadily. 'What we have found together is something we had no choice over. I couldn't stop myself falling in love with you and you couldn't stop it either. That spark was there from the very first moment. Our wedding was a farce but our marriage doesn't have to be. I have no idea how we will make it work but I know we can because what we have is too special to throw away. I never in a million years expected to feel like this about anyone and yet here we are. Give us a chance. Please, don't turn your back on something we could both search for another million years and never find.'

When she lifted her face to him, tears were streaming down her face. That was the moment Gianni knew he'd lost.

Chin wobbling manically, she shook her head and choked, 'I *can't*. You must understand that.'

He had no idea how he was able to keep his voice even. 'I understand that we love each other.'

'Stop saying that, it only makes it harder. We can never be. I can't betray Amelia. You have to go back to your own life and let me go back to mine.'

'Amelia betrayed *you*.'

She shook her head violently. 'No. Never.'

'She lied to you. You know it in your heart.'

'No! She wouldn't! And even if she did, she would have had her reasons. Oh… You don't understand!'

'Then make me. Tell me. Tell why you are so ready to throw us away.'

'I don't want to throw us away! I want to be with you but it's impossible.'

'Explain it to me. You owe me that much.'

'Gianni… You said I don't hold bitterness and anger towards my mother, and that I learned to understand and forgive her and help her…none of that came easy. There were times I *hated* my mum for what she was doing to herself but I never let myself fall into despair because through it all, I had my sister. I have looked up to her my entire life, even when I was a brat to her in the days when I believed everything was perfect. Amelia's the one who held what was left of our family together and held me together. She's the one who helped Mum, not me; I only helped Amelia help her. She's the one who protected me from the bullies at the horrid school we were sent to after Dad...' She cut herself off and took a long breath before looking him squarely in the eye. 'I know dad ripped you off. I believe you. If you say he ripped off other companies and people too then I believe you. And if you say Amelia lied to me about finding proof of corruption against you then I believe that too.'

Oh, but it *hurt* to finally admit that, and Issy had to wipe away more tears before adding, 'I believe you, Gianni. She lied to me.'

God help her, she was taking Gianni's word over her own sister's. But she knew it. From the moment he'd denied it, she'd known in her heart, just as he'd said, that he was telling the truth. It was a truth she'd locked away from herself in the beautiful days they'd just shared, burying it because she'd fallen madly in love and had selfishly wanted to have this time with him, because he was right about that too—what she felt for him would never be replicated.

All along though, she'd known it would have to end. What she hadn't known was how much it would hurt.

'You believe me?' He grabbed the back of his neck and sucked air in.

'It doesn't change anything. She hates you and your cousin too much. Her lie must have been born out of desperation, there's no other explanation for it. You should have seen her in the days leading up to my leaving for the Caribbean; she was so tense at the thought our time was finally coming that I thought she would snap. That we've failed will be destroying her. I can't add to that. I just can't. I can't betray her.'

'You already have,' he stated flatly.

'I know.' God, she was going to cry again. 'But this…here…what we've shared…soon it will be just a memory. For me to leave her and make a life with you… It would devastate her. She would never forgive me.'

'Do you not think it is the same for me?'

Taken aback at the tightness in his voice, Issy met his stare. The coldness shining from his eyes made her quail.

'Do you not think Alessandro will think I have betrayed him? Me, the one person in this world he trusts, falling in love with one of the women who set out to destroy us?' The more he spoke, the more the ice-like fury that had been building in Gianni while Issy had been making all her excuses spread. 'Me, falling in love with Thomas Seymore's daughter and wanting to build a life with her? Do you not think that will land like a kick in the teeth to him? And do not forget, Alessandro is as much of a victim in this whole charade as I am. More so. While you and I have been having fun here in the Caribbean, he's been fighting for the very existence of our company. Don't you think I know what the consequences could be? Exactly the same as what you fear. The difference is I love you enough that I'm willing to lose everything to be with you. I would walk on hot coals for you, but you…' He laced his voice with all the contempt he could inject into it. 'You're a coward. You won't even try, and you're using your sister as an excuse.'

She looked like he'd slapped her. 'How can you say that? You know what we've been through and what we mean to each other.'

'That's my whole point,' he spat. 'If your sister loves you as much as you love her then she will want the best for you. She will want you to be happy. If you wanted it enough, you would convince her. I don't deny she will be angry and betrayed but in time she would come round. Maybe she would never accept me as a brother-in-law but she sure as hell wouldn't want to lose you, but we will never know, will we? And I will never know if Alessandro would forgive me because you're so scared that I'll end up abandoning you as your parents did through their addictions that you'd rather cling to your sister's skirt and use her as an excuse than take the leap of faith with me.'

'I'm not scared,' she whispered.

'Liar.' Rising to his feet, he dusted the sand from his hands. 'And so much for trusting me.'

Unable to bear looking at her stricken, cowardly face a moment longer, Gianni turned on his heel and walked away from her.

'Where are you going?' Issy scrambled to her feet, panic suddenly clawing at her.

'To call Captain Caville. The *Palazzo delle Feste*'s moored on an island fifty kilometres away. It will not take long to reach us. I suggest you start packing.'

She had to practically run to catch him. 'What, we're leaving?'

'I have no wish to stay here another minute longer than necessary.'

'But we're not expected back in London for a couple more days.'

'Our time here is over.'

'Please, Gianni, don't let it end like this.'

He came to an abrupt halt and spun around to face her. 'What the hell do you expect? A few more days of *fun* together? No, you have made your decision and I have made mine. We will sail to the nearest island with an airport that flies to the UK and I will buy you a ticket for the first flight home.'

'And what about you?' she asked, almost numb with shock at his implacable coldness.

'That, *bella*—' he virtually spat the endearment '—is none of your business. My lawyer will be in touch over the dissolution of our *marriage...*' There was even more venom in his voice. 'Do not expect anything from me. This marriage meant nothing. *We* meant nothing. Enjoy your life.'

When his long legs set stride again, Issy let him go.

CHAPTER FOURTEEN

Issy sat on the balcony of her cabin on the *Palazzo delle Feste* gazing up at the stars. There were so many of them twinkling down on her from the moonless sky. She wished they injected warmth as far as Earth. Despite the balminess of the night she was huddled under the wrap she'd packed for the unpredictable weather when she returned to London. She'd felt chilled to the bone since Gianni had so coldly and ruthlessly severed her from his life.

And it had been a severing. A member of staff had collected her suitcase from her chalet and walked her to the yacht. Since embarking, she hadn't caught a glimpse or heard a whisper from Gianni. She'd wandered aimlessly through the familiar rooms, half hoping and half dreading bumping into him. She'd even knocked on his cabin door and still didn't know if she'd been relieved or devastated that it went unanswered. She'd tried the handle but it had been locked. Probably for the best. She didn't know what she'd have said to him.

He must have had a change of heart and stayed behind on St Lovells.

Maybe it was better this way. A clean break. It would have happened in a few days anyway. It was just in the few times she'd envisaged it—only brief visions, because nausea had roiled strongly inside her at the images in her mind's eye—they had parted with tender words. She'd imagined a life spent weaning herself off her internet addiction to him.

She pulled the wrap tighter around her shoulders and wished she could call Amelia, tell her she knew what she'd done but that it didn't matter because whatever reason had propelled her sister to act so out of character and lie to her must have been important. The more she thought about it, the more it hurt her heart that Amelia hadn't felt able to confide that reason in her.

But she couldn't call her. In the days of bliss when she'd been blocking the world from her head, she'd left her phone in Gianni's dressing room. To take it back would have let the world intrude and she'd been desperate to avoid that. And then everything had crumbled between them and she'd hidden in her chalet until the call to leave had come. She'd been too numb to think about anything.

She wished she was still numb. Now, she felt sick to the pit of her stomach and it hurt even more to know that even if she had remembered her phone, she'd not be able to confide any of the pain she was feeling to her sister.

Or would she?

Gianni's cold voice kept echoing like a taunt in her ear. *Coward.*

How was she being a coward? And as for his ridiculous assertion that she had abandonment issues?

A spark of fury suddenly fired in her. If she did have abandonment issues—which she didn't—hadn't his behaviour proved her right to have them? And just like that, the coldness left her. Jumping to her feet, Issy paced her balcony, wishing Gianni was on board so she could confront him with the home truths she wished she'd thought of earlier. That it was grossly unfair to call her a coward just because she put her sister's feelings above her own. That if he thought she had abandonment issues, at least she didn't cut the abandoner from her life even if they did deserve it, which Gianni's mother undoubtedly did. That…that…that…

The stars began to blur. And then they began to spin.

Dazed, Issy staggered back to her seat and breathed deeply, waiting for the dizziness to pass.

But it didn't pass, just built up and up more and more as the truth rose in her stomach and chest and up her throat and she had to cover her mouth to stop the agony escaping.

She *was* a coward. Of *course* Amelia would forgive her. Maybe not overnight but in time she would, just as Issy would forgive her anything, even lying to her about something so dangerous as the Rossi cousins.

Gianni wasn't dangerous. Not in the way she'd once believed. He was dangerous in the way he could sever a relationship without batting an eyelid. Issy had obsessed over him and witnessed from afar his litter of broken hearts for so many years that taking that final leap—what had he called it? A leap of faith?—had been too terrifying to contemplate. Because her parents' addictions *had* felt like abandonment, like she wasn't enough to keep them sober and on this earth with her. Not even enough to keep her mother in the country with her. Yes, she'd long ago accepted it and forgiven them both for it but it had done something to her she hadn't even realised and so when the chance had come to give herself properly, heart, body and soul to Gianni, she'd cowered in fright because deep down she was so goddam scared he would leave her too. And so she had pushed him away before he could push her and now the truth was demanding she confront it, and she realised he never would have. Gianni would never have left her. It wasn't that she had tamed the lothario or anything clichéd like that, but a magical alchemy of chemistry and passionate desire sprinkled with a meeting of minds and humour had captured them and woven their hearts together. They belonged together.

And she'd thrown it away. Been too frightened to take what he was so gladly offering.

No wonder he'd been so cold and furious. For the first time since his mother had abandoned him, Gianni had handed his heart over on a plate and Issy had rejected it.

In the distance the dark shadow of approaching land appeared and it was the knowledge that on that island sat the airport from which she would take the flight that would fly her away from him that finally broke her.

Sliding off the chair, Issy fell onto her knees with a thump, opened her lungs and howled.

Gianni had been sat on his balcony for over two hours hardly daring to breathe in case Issy heard him. He'd cursed to hear her step out on her balcony, cursed himself too for not putting her in a cabin far from his.

He wanted nothing to do with her, not even a glimpse of her, and when she'd knocked on his door he'd taken great pleasure in ignoring her. What the hell did she even want with him?

And now he was trapped on his balcony waiting for her to do the decent thing and go back inside so he could wallow in the bottle of Jack he'd brought out here for company.

Movement came. Great! She must be going inside.

No, she was stomping around, which was unusual as she had such a light, graceful tread to her step.

Dammit, all he wanted was to wallow until he reached the bottom of the bottle and be drunk enough not to notice when the yacht docked and Issy disembarked for the final time from his life. He was going to sail on to Barbados and take his jet back to London from there. It was safer that way. No risk of accidentally bumping into her.

She stopped stomping. Excellent.

He folded his arms across his chest and waited impatiently for her to finally disappear inside. Except there was no obliging sound of a door being slid open or closed.

A loud thud made him jump to his feet.

What the hell...?

But the thought had barely formed when an animalistic howl of agony rent the air.

'Issy?' he shouted, rushing to the barrier separating their balconies. Dammit, why the hell had he insisted the barrier be high enough for complete privacy? He called her name again but the only sound from her balcony was heart-wrenching sobs. 'Stay where you are,' he ordered, trying not to let the panic that she'd seriously injured herself consume him. 'I'm coming.'

Racing through his cabin, he yanked his door open and ran straight to Issy's door, praying she hadn't locked it. God answered that one, and he pushed it open before racing to her balcony door and sliding that open too.

What he found stopped him in his tracks.

Issy was curled on the floor in the foetal position, great sobs racking her entire body.

In an instant he was beside her and hauling her into his arms so she was cradled on his lap.

'Where are you hurt?' he asked urgently. 'Please, *mia amore*, tell me where you're hurt.'

Slowly it dawned on Issy that she wasn't dreaming. Hallucinating Gianni's voice had been more than she could endure and she'd covered her ears like a child against the cruelty of it, crying so hard her ribs felt bruised.

She hadn't hallucinated it. She hadn't hallucinated him.

Tentatively, still afraid he would disappear in a

blink, she touched his cheek. It was as warm and solid as it always was but still she whispered, 'Gianni?'

'Tell me where it hurts,' he repeated in the same urgent tone that had finally cut through her despair.

'Hurts?' she echoed.

'You have hurt yourself. You are in pain.' His Italian accent was stronger than she had ever heard it. 'Please, you must tell me where it hurts.'

More tears streamed down her face as her hand fluttered to her chest and pressed against her left breast. Against her heart. 'Here.'

'What have you done?'

'Pushed you away.'

He didn't understand.

'Oh, but I'm the biggest fool in the world.' Trembling, she cupped both his cheeks tightly. 'Please forgive me. Please give me another chance. Please don't give up on me and cut me from your life. I couldn't bear it. I *can't* bear it. I love you, Gianni, and I want to build a life with you.'

He hardly dared believe what her lips were saying and her eyes were pleading.

'It's not even been ten hours since you walked away from me and they've been the longest ten hours of my life. What we have found together…you're right. I could walk this earth for a million years and never find it again.'

'And your sister?'

'She loves me. She'll forgive me in her own time, but right now it's you I need forgiveness from.'

'Mia amore…' A bubble of hope was starting to

build inside him. 'There is nothing for me to forgive. I didn't react as well as I should and lashed out at you and for that, I am sorry too.' He took a deep breath before admitting, 'I think I have a problem with rejection.'

Her chin wobbled but she managed a smile. 'A small one, maybe.'

He raised an eyebrow which made her smile widen and a small laugh escape her lips, and then before he even knew it was happening, her arms were wrapped around his neck, his hold around her had tightened and they were kissing with such passion and love that the bubble of hope exploded in a blaze of joy so strong that the last of Gianni's fears abandoned him.

'Your reaction was understandable,' she murmured when they came up for air. 'We both have abandonment issues.'

'Had,' he corrected, kissing her again. 'But not any more. You love me and you'll never let me go.'

'And you love me and will never let *me* go.'

'Never.'

'Never.'

And they never did.

Issy stretched luxuriously within the silk sheets of Gianni's bed…*her* bed…and yawned widely. She loved this room. This bed. This penthouse. She'd only spent two nights in it but already she felt at home. Gianni had made it feel like home for her.

The only thing that stopped Issy feeling like she could spring to the clouds in a single leap was dread about what was to come when Amelia finally arrived back home. Gianni had given her phone back to her and when she'd checked it, there hadn't been a single message or voice mail from her sister. Just a wall of silence. In a way, that had made it easier for her to maintain her own silence too, especially when Gianni's contacts had quickly confirmed she was still abroad with Alessandro.

When the bedroom door opened, she sat up, a smile already on her face at the joy that fizzed through her at the mere anticipation of seeing her husband—it was taking some getting used to, actually thinking of him as her husband—after being separated from him for fifteen whole minutes while he made them eggs for breakfast. One look at his face and empty hands wiped the smile away.

'What's happened?' she asked.

He shook his head and sat next to her to stroke her hair. 'Alessandro has sent me a message.'

Issy's heart thumped. Like her, Gianni had been waiting for his cousin's return to London before telling him about their marriage. 'He knows about us?'

'I'm not sure but that isn't why he messaged me. He's asked me to bring you to the airfield.'

'Why?'

Sympathy lined his face. 'Amelia's flying back to the UK. Alessandro says…he says she needs you.'

It was like ice had been injected into her veins. As sisters, they'd pulled together and always been there for one another emotionally, but Amelia had never *needed* her.

Gazing into the steadfast eyes of the man she still couldn't quite get her head around was her husband, bone-deep certainty grew that her sister was in great distress.

'You'll come with me?' she whispered.

Strong arms wrapped around her and held her close. *'Mia amore*, I would follow you to the ends of the earth.' He kissed her gently. 'I'll call our driver. We can leave in ten minutes.'

Our driver. *We.* Simple words but words infused with meaning.

It was the two of them. Together. For always.

EPILOGUE

GIANNI CLOSED HIS eyes contentedly as he swayed gently on the hammock under the rising early sun. Snuggled on him, his chubby cheek pressed against his chest, his youngest son, Matteo, slept. At only eighteen months, the little ratbag—an affectionate term Gianni's beautiful wife called him—had recently mastered the art of escaping his cot. That morning he had toddled into his parents' bedroom and woken Gianni by prodding his nose. With the rest of his family sleeping, Gianni had taken him outside to watch the sunrise.

He tried not to sigh to think that soon they would have to return to Europe. Mia, their eldest child, was a couple of weeks away from starting school. They'd debated whether to employ a tutor so they could continue spending six months of each year in their Caribbean hideaway but decided that would be selfish of them. As far as they were both concerned, children needed playmates. St Lovells would be there for all the school holidays and then, when their brood had all flown the nest, they would make it their permanent home. At least, that was the plan. How long it would take for that to happen was anyone's guess, a thought reinforced when a sound made him peer through one eye and spot his heavily pregnant wife sneaking towards him, carrying a huge, elaborately wrapped box, Mia bringing up the rear with carefully balanced, much smaller boxes in her own tiny hands.

His family. God, he loved them. Sometimes he would look at his children's happy faces and his heart would squeeze so tightly it left a bruise. Sometimes he would look at his wife and take in her flowing dark chestnut hair and curvy body and those beautiful blue eyes that always shone with such love, and thank every deity he could think of for bringing them together. Six years of marriage and their devotion to each other had only grown. She was his entire world. Their children were their universe.

'Happy birthday, Daddy!' Mia suddenly yelled.

He opened his eyes fully and feigned surprise.

Matteo lifted his head and grinned at him. ''Ap Birfday.'

Pressing his son's button nose, Gianni then held him tightly and swung himself off the hammock. Issy was beaming at him. The box was practically as tall as she was.

'Happy birthday, you gorgeous man. Bet you can't guess what your present is...*don't* tell him, Mia!'

Watching his daughter carefully place the other boxes on the table, he pretended to ponder. 'Hmm. Whatever can it be?'

Issy's beam grew.

Somehow they managed to exchange Matteo for

the box, and then Gianni ripped the wrapping, already grinning, imagining what she'd come up with this time.

It was a banana float. At least, that's what Gianni and Issy called it. Every year she brought him the same thing for his birthday. He was growing quite the collection. But each was decorated in its own unique way and he burst out laughing when he pulled it out of the box and found it had been cleverly painted with caricatures of his wife and two children's faces squashed together.

Placing it against the tree the hammock was tied to, he wrapped his arms around her as much as Matteo in her arms would allow, and kissed her deeply. 'Thank you,' he murmured.

'My pleasure,' she murmured back, before dropping her voice to a whisper. 'You can have the rest of your present when the children go to bed.'

He snapped his teeth with a mock growl and squeezed her delectable bottom. 'I look forward to it.'

'Stop being soppy and open our presents!' Mia demanded, spoiling the moment in the best possible way.

Laughing even harder, he scooped his daughter up and planted an enormous kiss to her cheek.

Not a day went by when Gianni didn't consider himself the luckiest man alive.

* * * * *

#4097 A BABY TO MAKE HER HIS BRIDE
Four Weddings and a Baby
by Dani Collins

One night is all Jasper can offer Vienna. The people closest to him always get hurt. But when Jasper learns Vienna is carrying his baby, he must take things one step further to protect them both... with his diamond ring!

#4098 EXPECTING HER ENEMY'S HEIR
A Billion-Dollar Revenge
by Pippa Roscoe

Alessandro stole Amelia's birthright—and she intends to prove it! Even if that means working undercover at the Italian billionaire's company... But their off-limits attraction brings her revenge plan crashing down when she discovers that she's carrying Alessandro's baby!

#4099 THE ITALIAN'S INNOCENT CINDERELLA
by Cathy Williams

When shy Maude needs a last-minute plus-one, she strikes a deal with the one man she trusts—her boss! But claiming to date ultrarich Mateo drags Maude's name into the headlines... And now she must make convenient vows with the Italian!

#4100 VIRGIN'S NIGHT WITH THE GREEK
Heirs to a Greek Empire
by Lucy King

Artist Willow's latest high-society portrait is set to make her career. Until the subject's son, Leonidas, demands it never see the light of day! He's everything she isn't. Yet their negotiations can't halt her red-hot reaction to the Greek...

#4101 BOUND BY A SICILIAN SECRET
by Lela May Wight

Flora strayed from her carefully scripted life and lost herself in the kisses of a Sicilian stranger. Overwhelmed, she fled his bed and returned to her risk-free existence. Now Raffaele has found her, and together they discover the unimaginable—she's pregnant!

#4102 STOLEN FOR HIS DESERT THRONE
by Heidi Rice

After finding raw passion with innocent—and headstrong—Princess Kaliah, desert Prince Kamal feels honor-bound to offer marriage. But that's the last thing independent Liah wants! His solution? Stealing her away to his oasis to make her see reason!

#4103 THE HOUSEKEEPER AND THE BROODING BILLIONAIRE
by Annie West

Since his tragic loss, Alessio runs his empire from his secluded Italian *castello*. Until his new housekeeper, Charlotte, opens his eyes to the world he's been missing. But can he maintain his impenetrable emotional walls once their powerful chemistry is unleashed?

#4104 HIRED FOR HIS ROYAL REVENGE
Secrets of the Kalyva Crown
by Lorraine Hall

Al is hired to help Greek billionaire Lysias avenge his parents' murders...by posing as a long-lost royal *and* his fiancée! But when an unruly spark flares between them, she can't shake the feeling that she *belongs* by his side...

YOU CAN FIND MORE INFORMATION ON UPCOMING HARLEQUIN TITLES, FREE EXCERPTS AND MORE AT HARLEQUIN.COM.

HPCNMRB0323

HARLEQUIN
PLUS

Try the best multimedia
subscription service for romance
readers like you!

Read, Watch and Play.

Experience the easiest way to get
the romance content you crave.

Start your **FREE TRIAL** at
<u>www.harlequinplus.com/freetrial</u>.